Girl in a Cage

Girl in a Cage

JANE YOLEN

& ROBERT J. HARRIS

SCHOLASTIC INC.

New York Toronto London Auckland Sydney
Mexico City New Delhi Hong Kong Buenos Aires

ISBN 0-439-59177-5

Copyright © 2002 by Jane Yolen and Robert J. Harris. All rights reserved.
Published by Scholastic Inc., 557 Broadway, New York, NY 10012,
by arrangement with Philomel Books, an imprint of Penguin Putnam Books for Young Readers
a division of Penguin Group (USA) Inc. SCHOLASTIC and associated logos
are trademarks and/or registered trademarks of Scholastic Inc.

12 11 10 9 8 7 6 5 4 3 2   3 4 5 6 7 8/0

Printed in the U.S.A.   40

First Scholastic printing, October 2003

Book design by Semadar Megged

The text is set in 12-point Horley Old Style.

TIMELINE

1274   Birth of Robert the Bruce.

1286   Death of Alexander III of Scotland.

1290   Death of the Maid of Norway.
Edward I of England, known as Longshanks, is invited to judge the candidates for King of Scotland.

1292   Edward chooses John Balliol, who is crowned King of Scotland.

1295   Marjorie Bruce born.
After defying Edward I, King John Balliol is imprisoned in England.

1296   John Balliol (Toom Tabard) abdicates, goes into exile in France.
Edward I declares himself King of Scotland.

1297   Death of Robert Bruce's first wife, Isabel of Mar.
William Wallace defeats the English at the Battle of Stirling Bridge.

1298   Edward I defeats William Wallace at the Battle of Falkirk.

1302   Robert Bruce submits to Edward I and marries Elizabeth de Burgh.

1305   William Wallace is captured and executed by the English.

1306   February: Robert Bruce kills John Comyn in Dumfries.
March: Robert Bruce is crowned King of Scotland.
June: Battle at Methven near Perth.
August: Robert Bruce arrives at Strathkillan.
Fights the MacDougalls at Dalry.
September: Kildrummy Castle besieged.
October: Marjorie Bruce taken prisoner to England.

1 ☞ THE FIRST DAY OF MY CAPTIVITY

Dear Lord, if it is not too much to ask, could you please send less wind and fewer turnips?

The wind rattles the iron bars of my cage making me shake like an old man at his prayers.

As for the turnips, the good folk of Lanercost should rather eat them than throw them at me. It would be better for all our souls.

If Father is ever king in more than name, I shall remember those turnips.

And the people who threw them.

I have measured out the dimensions of my prison and it is only four paces on each side. When I jump up, I can brush the ceiling with my fingertips, so I estimate the cage to be seven feet in height.

The floor is of bare wood with neither rug nor scattering of rushes to soften it. There are no furnishings, no chair, not even as much as a stool. There is no wash basin or cloth.

One corner of the cage has been concealed behind a plain, sackcloth curtain. Drawing the curtain aside, I find a crude privy that consists only of a bucket.

I have been trying to persuade myself that this whole thing

is a cruel joke. That soon the English will be satisfied with their cleverness and take me inside the priory where the monks live. However humble a cell they might prepare for me, at least it would be away from the prying eyes of the vengeful country folk of Lanercost.

Now night comes, one of those soupy October eves. My tormentors have gone away at last, to warm stew and warmer beds than I, of that I am certain.

Through the moist air I can hear the monks singing vespers—evening prayers—in the chapel behind the walls. Their voices are deep and not very musical. I can't help wondering if any of them will bother to pray for me. Probably their king has forbidden it.

By the main gate, a soldier stands just out of earshot. Even were he close enough to hear me, he would not answer. King Longshanks has commanded silence.

The monks, too, have been forbidden speech with me. In fact, the only words I have heard all day have been insults from the crowd.

"Rebel!" they yelled.

"Traitor!"

They shouted other words, too, ones I had never heard before. I do not think I want to know what they mean. In fact, I can hardly think at all. All I seem to be able to do is lie here on the floor of the cage.

My whole body is shaking and my breath comes out in painful sobs. I do not want anyone to see me like this or to hear my crying. But there is nowhere to hide.

Surely I do not deserve this. I never hurt a soul. All I ever wanted to do was to read and ride and hawk and dance and play in the gardens at Lochmaben.

Why, only a few months ago, when Father was crowned and I was a princess, how foolish I was then. I remember how I had kissed Father and curtsied.

"My lord," I said. "King Robert de Brus of Scotland."

He had laughed, the skin crinkling up around his eyes. " 'Father' will do when we are alone, Marjorie."

And now I lie in a cage, shivering like a wild beast. My clothes are filthy, my nose a waterfall. And my spirit, if not broken, is at least bent like a reed in the troubling Autumn wind.

Dear Lord, never mind the turnips. Do something about the wind.

2 ❧ BERWICK, SOUTHERN SCOTLAND, OCTOBER 1306

The soldiers who surrounded me seemed embarrassed. So many of them needed to guard one small girl. I was not yet twelve and my waist was but a hand's span. I did not yet come up to a man's shoulder. Yet as we left the town of Berwick-upon-Tweed, there was a company of soldiers around me. All of them ordered to make sure that I got safely to Lanercost.

Lanercost!

Say, rather, Hell.

My guards were no happier than I to be going there.

I supposed the soldiers would rather have been chasing through the Highlands after my father and uncles and the few who follow them. But instead the Englishmen had to keep an eye on me.

On me.

Marjorie de Brus. Marjorie Bruce. The Scottish king's only daughter.

They stuck me in the back of a wagon, the floor of which was strewn with dirty straw. Its last load had left a rotten stink behind. Pigs perhaps. Or sheep. Longshanks' men had probably stolen the wagon from some poor farmer.

I tried to speak to the two soldiers who rode in the wagon with me. They were up front, driving the horses. I used my best manner. Though I had not been a princess for long, I *had* been an earl's daughter all my life, so I knew *some* things.

"This is not a proper carriage," I told them. "Can't you find a better one?"

All I could see of the driver and his companion were their peaked iron helmets and their leather tunics. One of them muttered something and the other one grumbled back.

"Speak up," I commanded.

They did not react, but kept their eyes on the horsemen leading the way.

"Where are we going?" I asked. When they did not respond, I repeated the question, slowly and loudly, as if talking to a simpleton. Or a Frenchman. "Where—are—we—going?"

After a long pause, the driver made a sound halfway between a grunt and a throat clear. "Lanercost."

His partner elbowed him. "Don't talk to her. King's orders."

That was the first I heard that Longshanks was taking personal interest in my capture.

That worried me some. But the silence worried me more. My nurse, Maggie, had used it when I was little, sending me off to my room when I was naughty, to think quietly on my sins. I had loathed it then. How much more would I loathe it now.

"She be but a girl," the driver said to his companion.

I was suddenly desperate to keep them talking. "Where is Lanercost?"

The driver half turned to look at me. He had a pleasant enough face—for an Englishman—with ruddy cheeks and a nose bulbed like a leek.

"England," he growled, scornful of my ignorance.

"Just barely," added the other, who was thinner, more like

the stalk of a leek. He sounded disappointed. I suppose he wanted to drive closer to his home, wherever that was.

"Is that where they are taking my stepmother?" I asked.

There was no reply.

"What about my aunt Mary? And where is my uncle Neil?"

Silence.

"What has happened to Countess Isabel and the Duke of Atholl?"

Still nothing.

Their silence began to grate. I might be only a prisoner in a dirty wagon to them, but I was still a princess. And a princess is entitled to common courtesy at least.

"Will you not answer?" My voice sounded shriller than I intended.

"It's *you* that will answer, girl," Stalk snapped. He turned and bared his rotten teeth at me. "Answer to the king's justice. Until then, cease your prattling and give us peace."

His rebuke was so harsh, I flopped back as if I had been pushed.

The king's justice. He meant King Edward of England, of course. Longshanks. My father's sworn enemy.

"But . . ." I whispered, "I am just a child."

My father did not make war on children.

Obviously Edward Longshanks did.

3 ❧ LANERCOST, ENGLAND, OCTOBER 1306

When we stopped on the road at night they tied me by both arms and my left foot to a wheel of the wagon so that they could all get a good night's sleep without having to stand guard over me.

All night long I listened to their snores and coughs, their hawkings and farts. All night long the ropes chafed at my skin. And all night long a cold wind puzzled through the trees, catching me about the ears. I was afraid to wake the soldiers with my plaints lest that make things worse, though I doubted anything could be worse.

How little did I know.

How very little.

Before dawn I fell into a weary sleep, only to be wakened by a tugging on the rope.

"Let me at least go behind the bushes to relieve myself," I begged.

"Do it in the cart," one of the soldiers said.

So I did.

We arrived at Lanercost, just over the Scottish border, after a three-day bone-shaking journey. My nose was streaming and my arms and back ached. I was filthy and covered with insect bites.

But when I saw the great stone building with its towers and arches, with its orchards and gardens, I sighed. There was bound to be an apartment for me. Not a cozy room as I had back home, of course. I was a prisoner after all. But at least something befitting my station.

The captain of my escort helped me down from the wagon. He was a handsome man with a sharp, foxlike face. I smiled at him.

He did not smile back.

"What is this place?" I asked.

"Lanercost Priory." He spoke as if each word cost a fortune.

I knew a priory was a sort of monastery, so I supposed then that my lodgings would be *very* simple and spare. Monks, after all, take vows of poverty. Still, the building and grounds looked rich. The stone was well-dressed, and there were carvings above the arches. Then I remembered hearing gossip that the English monasteries were so rich the monks ate well in spite of their vows. That they had servants to tend their flocks and dig their peat and keep their kitchens.

Perhaps, I thought, this might not be such a bad place to wait until my father could get here. I knew he would. It was only a matter of time. He would pay ransom for me, or send a host of good Scots soldiers to free me.

I hoisted my filthy skirts, held my head high, and began walking toward the priory's vaulted entrance. The fox-face captain seized my arm and steered me away.

"What is it?" I said, gasping at his hard grip.

He did not answer, but instead dragged me toward the road that divided the priory from the village to the north.

A small platform had been raised there, about four feet high, and on top of it squatted a cage of latticed timber and iron. It looked as if it had been built to hold a bear, the kind that can be seen performing at fairs.

Another of the soldiers opened the door of the cage and the captain pulled me straight toward it.

The sudden realization that they meant to lock me inside overpowered me. The long ride in the open wagon, the mean-spirited drivers, my running nose and itchy bites, were mere insults to this. I was so shocked, I hardly struggled as they bundled me inside.

Then the heavy iron door clanged shut behind me.

A soldier with a wandering right eye fastened the lock and handed the key to the captain.

As they started walking away, my senses returned. I grabbed the thick bars in my hands and called out.

"You cannot mean to leave me here! This is all a terrible mistake. I am the king's daughter."

They paused and looked back. Then the captain burst into laughter, the tips of his red mustache bobbing. "Ned Long-shanks' daughter?" he said. "I think not."

"King Robert's daughter," I cried.

"Robert Bruce is no king," said the captain.

"He's a traitor to King Edward," said the soldier.

Then the two of them disappeared around the corner of the wall.

"My father . . . my father will punish you for this . . . " My voice trailed away. I knew the truth even as I tried to deny it. My father was far from here fighting his own battles, dodging among the mountains, fleeing the English king's long arm. He probably did not even know where I was. The only one who could wage a war here in Lanercost was I.

And I had nothing to wage it with.

I looked about my prison. A bare floor, cold metal bars. Nothing to keep out wind or weather. It was worse even than the wagon, which at least had had some straw.

Then I noticed a dozen villagers who had gathered to watch the soldiers. They were nudging each other, laughing, and pointing at me.

Surely they could see how cruel and unfair this was. Surely some of them would help.

They ambled toward me, forming a loose circle around the cage. There were eight men, some of them little more than boys, and four women. Most of them were old, their faces grey and bony. But old people were wise, surely.

"Fetch a judge, good people," I called out. "Get someone to release me. I am a princess of Scotland."

"Release ye?" one of the men mocked. He had a dirty line of hair over his upper lip less like a mustache and more like a scar. "Yer exactly where ye belong."

"It won't be long before *all* of ye Scots are in cages," said one old woman, laughing.

"Yer thieves and cutthroats, every one."

"Liars and robbers."

I could feel the blood draining from my face. No one had ever spoken to me like that in my entire life. Nor said such things about the Scots.

"But I have done nothing to you English," I said. "Nothing at all."

The oldest woman there, lower lip trembling, stepped forward and pointed a bony finger at me. "Ye Scots have raided us English for years. Come cross our border and stolen our cattle, murdered our men."

"Aye, burned and robbed, ye murdering reivers, but no more!" roared one of the men. He picked up a rock and threw it.

Jumping back, I tripped over my skirts and fell to the floor with a thud as the rock clanged off the bars of the cage. Horrified, I shrank away from the townsfolk.

The old woman who had just accused me of raiding and murder lunged forward. "Ye should burn for what ye've done," she screeched. "I lost a son to you savages!" I could smell ale on her breath all the way across the cage.

I wanted to tell her that I had never robbed or murdered anyone. That *she* was the savage, not I. But I did not get the chance.

One of the men laid an arm around her scrawny shoulders and drew her gently away. "Come, Mother, we've work to do. The Scottish king's daughter'll keep."

There was grumbling agreement and gradually the villagers drifted away.

4 ᘒ LOCHMABEN, SCOTLAND, FEBRUARY 1306

If my reckoning serves me right, it cannot have been more than eight or nine months ago that I was content in my household and certain of my place.

I have lived an entire life since then. I have been in royal banquets and in bloody fights. I have seen my father hailed as a king and chased as a bandit. I have danced at great houses and dodged arrows in green valleys. And all before my twelfth birthday.

I remember exactly the day things began to change, though who knew at the time the change was to be for the worse? We all thought things would be the better—for us and for our poor Scotland.

It was a typical February day and we were at Lochmaben Castle, my father's favorite place in the whole world.

And—usually—mine.

That day the rain was slating down, grey and cold. Everyone in the castle was in a foul mood.

Father had been gone for weeks, though this was not unusual. He was not any kind of king then, but was Earl of Carrick and Lord of Annandale. He owned lands and houses in Scotland. But he owned even more deep in England, many of which had come to him when he married my stepmother.

Having all of those houses meant he had to spend time visiting them. If he did not, he might have been cheated by an estate manager. Or an English neighbor might have schemed to grab off our land. Most important of all, Father had to keep on the good side of King Edward Longshanks because the English king was so moody, he often stole away the property of anyone to whom he took a dislike.

Knowing why Father had to be away did not help. I still missed him horribly, whatever the reasons.

When I had been very little, I had thrown temper tantrums each time he left home, or so my nurse, Maggie, told me. I fear I was not much better once I had grown. Each parting with him was still agony for me. And though I no longer flung myself prostrate on the ground, screaming or holding my breath till I turned an awful shade of blue, I was no angel about his absences either.

What had long made it worse was that Father had never once taken me with him when he went to visit his English estates. It was as if he were ashamed of me and did not want to show me off to the English royalty.

Uncle Neil finally explained Father's reasons to me. It seems that about the time I was born, Father had gotten into trouble with King Longshanks for supporting some Scottish rebels. Longshanks had demanded that Father hand me over to him as a hostage, to make sure Father behaved himself. "What could be a better guarantee than a man's own daughter?" Uncle Neil said.

Father had argued, pleaded, even flattered the king. He stalled in every way he could think of. Uncle Neil said he had finally told the king, "I will stand surety for my own behavior, sire," which I think must have been a very brave thing to say.

Uncle Neil had added, "There was no way he was going to let old Neddy Longshanks raise you."

At last the king simply forgave him. Father could be that charming. But, to this day, Father still had to visit the king on a regular basis. Just in case.

"To keep Longshanks sweet toward us," was how he put it before going off once again.

"I would the king were sweet to me," I had said, thinking only about royal balls and the great houses in England that I had never seen.

Both Father and Elizabeth, my stepmother, had turned as one and stared at me.

"Be careful what you would have," Elizabeth said. "That you not regret it later." Her lips had pulled into a thin, disapproving line.

That evening in February, with the rain drumming against the stone walls of Lochmaben's keep, I was in my apartments with Maggie. Though I was really already too old to have a nurse, Maggie remained as my servant and my friend. And no one nicer to spend a dull, dreary evening with when Father was away, except perhaps for Uncle Neil.

Maggie and I were sitting on cushions on the floor, snug by the fire, while the wind gusted outside. She was teaching me a new French song to sing to Father when he returned. He was due back any day.

The tune of the song was easy, but I couldn't get my tongue around some of the words.

"Och, the words dinna matter," Maggie assured me, her round face wreathed in smiles. "It is the sound of yer voice that will delight the earl's ears."

I was not so certain. I thought I really sounded like a thrush with a cough. As for the French—well, Maggie had no ear for it. She was Scots through and through, and mangled everything that was not in her own tongue. It was my stepmother from whom I was learning French, though practicing it with Maggie.

I started the song again feeling as if I were making my way across a rushing stream and those difficult words were the mossy stepping stones. I had made it as far as the last verse when the door opened and in came Elizabeth.

"Good evening, Stepmother," I said, for that was what I called her still, though she had been married to Father for four years.

Elizabeth's own father is the Earl of Ulster, one of the richest and most powerful nobles in all Ireland. At one time I had supposed she had come to the marriage with much money. It was Maggie, though, who told me that Father had married for love, not riches. The second time round as well as the first. As I knew we were already rich enough, perhaps she was right.

"You have long needed a mother," Maggie had added.

It is true I never had any mother that I remembered. Mine died soon after I was born, so how could I miss her? All I knew of her was her name—Isabel of Mar—and a few portraits on the stairs. She was a slim beauty with a high forehead and a calm smile. I looked nothing like her, being more Bruce than Mar, as everybody said. I was not even named for her, being Marjorie after my father's mother.

Still, I did not feel the loss of a mother. After all, I had Maggie, and she seemed quite enough.

As for Elizabeth, she seemed to have no interest in mothering me. She never hugged or kissed me the way Maggie did.

She did not come into my room when I had bad dreams or bring me a posset and sit by my bed when I had a fever. She did not compliment me and clap her hands with joy when I remembered a French verb or sang a difficult song or embroidered a particularly fine piece. I think she was hoping to have children of her own, certainly a boy child who would become earl after Father. But she was four years barren and that was not—as Maggie liked to say—a good sign.

A tall woman, Elizabeth was not exactly pretty. "Handsome" is what people called her. I think they admired her the way they admire the snowy peak of a mountain or the icy waters of a wide loch. A cold beauty. She had dark hair, thin lips, and winter eyes, the same color as Father's, the same color as mine. And sometimes we were mistaken for mother and daughter. But not for long. She always reminded any visitors who made such a mistake that she was far too young to have had me, though Maggie said that was not strictly true.

But true enough.

I thought at the time that Father and Elizabeth did not yet have a baby because they were still learning to love each other. When I said this to Maggie, she just laughed and answered, "They love each other plenty, my wee lass."

So there we were, Maggie and I, in front of the fire, when my stepmother came into my rooms and said, "It's getting late. Time you got this young lady off to bed."

"If I'm a lady," I had replied, "then I should stay up later. Can I come down and talk to my uncles awhile?"

"If you are ever to grow into a *proper* lady, then you must have your sleep," my stepmother said with a great sigh. She seemed to sigh a lot around me as if I made her tired.

"I'll get her off to bed," said Maggie obediently. "I was just teaching her a new song to please the earl."

Just then a sudden breeze swept a few droplets of rain into the room.

"Oh, it's a dreadful night," my stepmother declared. "Someone should have closed the shutters long ago." She cast a stern eye upon Maggie and strode toward the window.

"No!" I yelled, running to stop her. "Stepmother, please. I have been kept inside all day. I want to feel the air so I can pretend we are out in the woods hawking or sailing on the loch."

"Pretending feeds no bellies nor heals any wounds." She reached to pull the shutters closed, then stopped, her eyes fixed on the road below.

I stood on my tiptoes and peered over the ledge. There was the dull mass of the loch stretching away to the east. Galloping along the bank were two horsemen. Even through the dark and the rain I knew exactly who they were. One rode on a broad, grey gelding. The other sat a sturdy brown pony.

"Father!" I cried. "And his squire with him."

Before anyone could stop me, I had bolted out of the room and bounded down the narrow stairway to the great hall at the foot of the keep. When I rushed in, my father's four brothers—Edward, Neil, Thomas, and Alexander—all jumped up from the table where they were just beginning their supper.

Neil stepped into my path and swept me up in his arms.

"What is all the hurry, little Jo?" he asked. "Has your bed caught fire?"

"No, of course not, silly." I laughed into his handsome, smiling face. "Father is back!"

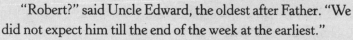

"Robert?" said Uncle Edward, the oldest after Father. "We did not expect him till the end of the week at the earliest."

Uncle Alexander laughed. "Never waste your time thinking Robert will do as you expect." They all nodded as he spoke, for Uncle Alexander is a brilliant scholar, one of the finest—'tis said—ever to graduate from Cambridge.

But now we could all hear the clatter of hooves in the court-yard, the voices of sentries and servants. And father's deep voice bellowing orders: to Will to take the horse and rub it down, to Duncan to clean up his sword, to Angus to tell Cook to bring him a big bowl of stew.

Then the great oaken door flew open with a bang and Father strode in. There was mud on his high boots and his cape was soaked with rain, but still that familiar fire lit his eyes, that no rain could put out.

"Father!" I tore from Uncle Neil's arms and ran to him.

He embraced me without care of getting me wet because he knew I would not mind. Then he hugged his brothers, throw-ing his arms around all of them at once as if they were puppies and not grown men.

They joked about his soaked clothes.

"We thought you might come back drunk, but never drowned," said Uncle Neil.

Everyone laughed at his jest, but my father went from laughing to stern in a second.

I pushed through the huddle of uncles to get close. Just as I reached his side, my stepmother spoke. "Robert, the child will be soaked through." She had just reached the foot of the stairs with Maggie behind her.

At the sound of her voice, Father turned and walked straight to her. He took her gently by the hands and kissed her cheek.

She dropped her eyes and I heard her whisper, "I am glad to see you home safe."

"Safe for now, at least," he answered her softly. Still holding one of her hands, he turned to face us all. "But I bring news that is not so happy. I have fallen afoul of the English king again, and this time the danger we have all feared is upon us at last."

My uncles all exchanged grim looks. Uncle Neil nervously turned his silver ring round and round his finger. Clearly they all understood what he was talking about, though I did not.

"What danger, Father?" I asked.

"Nothing that will ever imperil thee, poppet," he said gently in the old tongue.

5 ❧ LOCHMABEN, SCOTLAND, FEBRUARY 1306

I t is important that we discuss matters at once," Uncle Edward said, which brought on a great silence.

When I heard the word *important*, I knew what was going to happen next. So I slipped away, pretending I was leaving the room. But really—when no one was looking—I crouched down behind a chest in the corner, quiet as a mouse when the cat's about. It was the only way to learn anything in our household.

"Maggie, fetch the child upstairs," my stepmother commanded.

I could just imagine Maggie, a frown in the shape of an arrowhead between her brows. "I think she has gone upstairs already, my lady."

"Go and see," Stepmother ordered.

Maggie's skirts swept across the floor with a soft *swee-swash* as she scurried off toward the stairs.

"Thomas, secure the door," my father said.

From the sounds, I knew what was going on. Burly Uncle Thomas closed the door. There was a loud scraping of chairs and everyone sat down at table.

"Robert, this is no talk for women," Uncle Edward remarked dourly. He meant my stepmother.

I almost chuckled at the thought that Elizabeth might be sent away, while I remained here in secret.

"It is talk for all who are dear to me," Father said firmly.

That includes me, I thought, *so it is a good thing I am here.*

"Fill my cup for me, Alexander, and I will tell you all that has happened." Father's voice held some sort of misery that I could only guess at. After pausing for a sip of wine, he began his tale.

"A mere ten days ago, as you all know, I was at King Edward's court. An honored guest, or so I believed." He took another sip. "It is the last time I shall be any such thing."

"Have you done something rash?" my stepmother asked sharply. It was the same tone she used with me.

"If you call saving my neck rash," Father said.

I could hear her quick intake of breath.

He continued. "We Bruces are of the Scottish royal line and that has always put us in a dangerous position with the English king."

"Though John Balliol was chosen to rule instead of one of us." That was Uncle Edward, a hard edge to his voice.

"Aye, chosen by King Edward Longshanks," said Uncle Thomas. If anything the edge was harder in his voice.

"What does all that matter now?" Uncle Neil said. "Old Balliol abdicated the throne and languishes in exile in France. And his French has always been execrable." He laughed. *"Mon Doo, mon-sewer,"* he drawled in terrible French, much worse than Maggie's. He laughed again, this time at his own bad joke. I adored that laugh. It always made me giggle and I had to put my hand over my mouth to keep from making a sound. "He gave up Scotland's throne and gave it back to the English king. Balliol is an empty husk."

"Aye!" The uncles agreed as one.

"Aye," Father said. "Balliol is no threat. And you all know

that even *before* his abdication, I did all I could to keep the Bruce lands intact and away from English hands."

"We know all that, brother," Uncle Edward said. "Why cook a bannock that's already been eaten?"

The thought of a bannock made my mouth suddenly water. But I knew what Uncle Edward meant: Why waste time talking about something already done?

"Because it is important that you all understand what has happened," Father told him bluntly. There was a loud bang. Father must have slammed his fist on the table. "I have not only been visiting my properties, but gathering our forces and building alliances for the day when Scotland will rise once again. For the day when she will have a real king, not just an English puppet."

"Robert—what have you done?" Stepmother's voice rose to a whine, like a worried child.

For a long moment, no one spoke. At last Uncle Alexander said quietly, "I thought we had agreed nothing should happen till after King Edward dies, Rob. Under his rule, the English are too strong."

"And they say he is a sick man with no more than a year or two of life left," Uncle Thomas added.

"That *had* been our hope," Father agreed. "Scotland has never had a more ruthless foe than Edward Longshanks. He believes Scotland will lie under the English boot heel forever."

Uncle Alexander's quiet voice put in, "But his son is no Longshanks."

"His son," Uncle Neil said, "is a coward and an idiot. No one in the English army will follow *him*."

"Which is why we agreed to wait for Longshanks to die. So, why are you gathering strength *now*, Robert?" Uncle Alexander asked.

There was another silence. I waited as long as I could before peeking out from my hiding place to see what was going on.

Fortunately nobody was looking my way. Their eyes were all fixed firmly on Father.

People's eyes usually were.

It was not just that he was tall and handsome. So are all the uncles, especially Uncle Neil. But Father had something else, a way of moving with catlike grace, like a lion, I expect. And a way of making people love and trust him. Not the way I love him, of course, or Elizabeth loves him. But the way one loves a leader, or a king.

Father finished eating and slashed a napkin at his mouth. "In spite of Balliol's cowardice," he said finally, "there are Scots who continue to support him. Chief among these is my old rival, John Comyn."

"Red Comyn?" Uncle Neil gave a short laugh. "That gowk?"

"Not a gowk, not a fool, no," Father told him. "Rather, a thorn in the foot. I long believed that there could be no successful uprising unless Comyn and I came to some agreement, so I approached him some months ago, to discuss what we should do in the event of Edward's death. I even offered him all the Scottish lands I hold in Annandale and Carrick if he were to support me as king."

"Robert, not *all* the lands," my stepmother said.

"*All*, my love. The matter of kingship is more important than a few estates, no matter how lovely or well-seated." Father's chair scraped back. "I believed I had Comyn's agreement at the time."

"*Believed . . . ?*" Uncle Neil said. "What has changed?"

Father's face grew dark. "At this last visit to England, King Edward expressed doubts about my loyalty, even to my face."

"You would have been safer treading your way through a den of hungry lions," exclaimed Uncle Neil.

Father nodded. "So it proved. Ten nights ago, in Edward's court, it was made clear to me just *how* serious the danger was. I received a message from one of our father's old friends that Longshanks had been receiving reports about me, calling me a traitor. From Comyn."

"That treacherous worm!" Uncle Edward exclaimed hotly, surging to his feet and grasping the hilt of his sword.

Father waved him down. "Hold, Ned. The time for swords will be soon enough. It seems that Longshanks said—half in jest—that he might arrest me in the morning and seek out the truth of these accusations. I knew then I had no time to lose. Many a good and true man has confessed untruths under torture. Fleeing that very night with my squire, I rode full speed for Scotland and home."

"What now?" cried Uncle Neil. "You can't just sit here and wait for Edward to summon you."

"Or come after you with an army," Uncle Alexander added.

Father put his hands on Elizabeth's. "No, but first I must take steps to protect all of you, who are dearer to me than my life. And then . . . " He nodded at them each in turn. "Then, I must confront Comyn."

Uncle Thomas cleared his throat. "Comyn is close by, Rob, at a meeting of the justices in Dumfries."

"Does he realize Robert knows of his treachery?" Elizabeth asked.

"Probably not," Father said. "I have spoken of it to no one but you in this room. I will send a messenger this very night inviting him to meet me tomorrow in Greyfriars Abbey. I will surely learn then whether he repents of his actions, and if we are to be allies or foes."

"Can you trust him, whatever he says?" Uncle Edward asked.

"Trust a Comyn?" Uncle Neil answered for Father. "Rather trust an adder."

There was another long silence and I sank down again behind the chest wondering what it all meant.

For me.

For all of us.

My stepmother broke the silence, saying, "So, you will be king, Robert, whatever the cost?" There was a tremor in her voice that surprised me. Usually she sounded so sure of herself.

"I will be king," Father agreed, his voice strangely calm, "for without a king, Scotland will suffer the tyranny of the English forever." Then he said in a much lighter tone, "Now, my dear, please fetch that little girl out of her hiding place and see her off to bed."

My jaw dropped and I sat up.

Father was gazing directly upon me. I had no choice but to walk out in full view of everyone and surrender myself.

Uncle Neil tried to stifle his grin but the other uncles did not look so pleased. My stepmother looked positively grim.

"You deceitful child," she said. "You have no business here."

My father put his hand on her arm tenderly. "She has a useful knack for stealth, my dear," he said. Then he drew me into his embrace, stroking my hair. "And a positive genius for sticking to her position. One day she may need it."

My stepmother towed me upstairs to my rooms, where she dismissed Maggie and then tucked me in to bed personally.

"You are to forget what you heard tonight," she said. "And tell no one."

"Not even Maggie?"

"Especially not Maggie," she answered. "Now close your eyes and get a good night's rest." All unexpectedly, she bent down and pressed her cheek against mine. When she stood up there was a tiny tear glistening in one eye.

Little as I cared for her, it still disturbed me to see her cry.

"You should be happy," I told her. "You are going to be a queen and I am going to be a princess."

"Yes, I know," she sighed as she turned away. "And may God have mercy on us both."

6 ❧ THE SECOND DAY OF MY CAPTIVITY

It is barely morning and already there is another crowd. This time they are better prepared. They have rotten apples to throw as well. Only a few are able to fire their missiles through the bars of the cage, but all of them can aim their words like poisoned darts.

"Little animal!" they call me.

"Murderer's daughter!"

"Traitor's child!"

I bear their hatred as best I can, but I cannot help but flinch when they make a mock charge at my cage. They laugh and one redhead picks a pimple on his nose and flicks the discharge at me.

Is this English justice? No charges, no trial, just a dirty cage and a howling mob. I did not believe any people could be so heartless.

Crouching down on the yellow wood floor, I bury my face in my arms. I can still hear the voices, still hear the smack of rotten fruit against the bars, but I am no longer here. Instead, I am home, in Lochmaben, riding behind Uncle Neil on his great grey mare.

Uncle Neil!

Surely father will send him to rescue me. He will cut through these jeering peasants with a flash of his sword and then bend the bars of my cage with his bare hands. He will place his silver ring with the engraved thistle on my finger, the middle one else it will be too big. Then I will sit behind him and we will go galloping back to Scotland, back to my father's kingdom.

Dear Lord, please make it so.

How long I lay in my dream state I do not know, but when I wake, the sun is straight overhead and warm.

"Thank you at least for the sun, Lord," I whisper. A plump little monk in a long grey robe comes out of the priory carrying a tray. He keeps his head bowed low as though he has to watch his feet to make sure he does not trip.

I sit up, a flicker of hope in my heart. After all, this is a man of God. It is his duty to be kind, to help the unfortunate. Surely he will have some word for me. Perhaps he is even bringing me porridge. Or better yet, the key to my cage.

When he reaches the cage, I smile at him, but he does not seem to notice. He sets the tray down on the narrow edge of the platform and lifts a metal flap I have not seen before.

Could this be the means of my escape?

I watch carefully as the flap goes up. It opens a gap about twelve inches wide and no more than six inches high. Surely not enough room for even the skinniest prisoner to squeeze through.

One small hope gone. I feel a twist in my bowels. I will not let myself feel lost.

The monk takes a small tin cup of water from the tray and slides it through to me along with a slice of dry, crusty bread. Hungry though I am, I ignore both and speak urgently to him.

"Brother," I whisper through the bars, "why have I been locked up like this?"

He bows his head, presenting me with his shiny tonsure, the round patch of shaved scalp that monks wear as a mark of humility. The scalp circle looks like a face with no features. Without glancing up, he lowers the metal flap and slowly shakes his head. I can not tell if he is answering me or letting me know that he is forbidden to speak. Then, picking up the tray, he turns around, and shuffles back toward the priory.

"My father is king of Scotland!" I call after him, my eyes misting over with fresh misery. "He will come for me! Then you will all be sorry."

Again the monk slowly shakes his head.

"He will come for me," I whisper. "And Uncle Neil with him."

I wait a long time before eating.

One hour.

Two.

Time means nothing when you are in a cage.

Eventually I break off one small piece of the bread and wash it down with a sip of water. I want to make the pitiful meal last. Except for gnawing on the edible parts of the turnips and apples, I have had nothing to eat. But if my captors think to humble me by starvation, they should not have thrown food.

My supper is over almost as soon as it had begun, but I have one thing left.

The tin cup.

I place it in the center of the cage.

"Cup," I address it, "I am a king's daughter."

It speaks no more than the monk, but I laugh as I look at it, a laughter that is very close to tears.

"He will come for me," I say to the cup, meaning Father. Meaning Uncle Neil.

Then I sit back down again as the last rays of the sun fade behind the eastern hills.

Pale yellow dots of light shine in the windows of the nearby cottages. How often I had visited such little huts on our estates with Maggie, bringing our people extra food from our table.

But no one is visiting me, except to curse and throw food. And now the north wind—an unwelcome visitor from my homeland—whistles through the bars of the cage.

Wrapping my cloak tightly around me, I lay down. What I now would give for a few handfuls of the wagon's filthy straw!

7 ❧ LOCHMABEN, SCOTLAND, FEBRUARY 1306

The night after Father came home to Lochmaben, the hard rain beating against our castle walls had given way, and the rising sun splashed a streak of gold over the waters of the loch. The very air seemed charged with energy, like a horse before battle.

For a moment on waking I could not think what made the world seem so bright and new. And then I remembered.

My father was going to be king of Scotland.

And I a princess.

I rose from bed and twirled around. A princess! I had never actually met one and now I was to *be* one.

Well—almost one. Until Father was crowned, I was just an earl's daughter in an earl's castle. I thought of how much grander a king's palace would be. I thought of people curtsying to me. I hoped for a few new dresses.

Perhaps I would even have a crown.

As soon as I had dressed and eaten my milk and porridge, I rushed off to find Father. There was so much about kings and princesses I needed to know. But he was not around. And then I remembered—he had probably already left to meet with Red Comyn in the abbey.

Only Uncle Neil was around, standing in the courtyard in his riding gear, looking handsome and shining and wonderful under the morning sun. One of the boys was bringing his horse, Grey Glennie, out of her stall.

"Has Father already gone?" I asked, my face flushed from running.

Uncle Neil gathered me up and swung me around. "Yes—off to Dumfries with the others," he said. "The justices are meeting and your father is going to speak to Comyn." He put me down and now my face was burning because Uncle Neil always made me go warm all over. He was my favorite uncle, indeed my favorite person in the whole world, except for Father.

He laughed at my red cheeks. "However, I wanted my best tunic, and my fool of a servant had taken it away for cleaning." He rubbed his head ruefully. "I will have to ride fast to catch up, little Jo."

"Oh, take me with you," I pleaded, grabbing him by the sleeve. "There is always a market in the town when the justices meet, and I could spend time there while Father and Comyn talk. And afterward, when Father has convinced Comyn of the rightfulness of his cause, we can all celebrate, for Father will be king."

Uncle Neil frowned, which was—Maggie liked to say—a cloud before the sun. "I dinna ken about that." He spoke in Scots like one of the servants and gave me a wink. "Robert never said you could come."

"Did he say I could *not?*" I countered. I could tell he was weakening. He knew from experience it was quicker to give in to me than get caught up in an argument.

"What about your mother?"

"Stepmother," I said automatically. "She will not mind. Besides, I have been saving my pennies. So you see, I could buy some new ribbons while I wait."

"You can think of ribbons at a time like this?" He tried to look stern but he was laughing.

I answered haughtily, "Should I not look my best if I am going to be a princess?" Then I laughed back, to show I was only playing.

He gave a resigned sigh. "Well, I can see you already know how to bend your subjects to your will, Princess. Get your riding cloak, and be quick about it."

Soon we were trotting through the woods toward Dumfries. I was sitting behind Neil and holding on to the back of his belt with both hands as he guided his Grey Glennie, southward.

"It will not be long before you are riding your own horse, guarded by a company of knights in mantles of mail," he said over his shoulder. "A princess of the blood."

"You are the only knight I need, Uncle Neil," I said.

He chuckled. "You will need a more impressive escort than just me once Robert is king. Aye—that will be a good time. Like the golden days of good King Alexander, who ruled when your father was a boy."

Good King Alexander. My father had more than once told me about him. And also how good King Alexander had lost his life when his horse stumbled off a cliff, plunging them both onto the rocks below. Because the king had had no son, the only one who could succeed him on the throne was his granddaughter Margaret. She was off in Norway where she was betrothed to the prince. On the voyage home to Scotland she died, leaving a vacant throne and an empty crown.

"Oh, Uncle Neil," I said, suddenly filled with a deep sadness, "the poor little maid of Norway." I put my head against his broad back. Even thinking about Margaret's death always made my eyes prickle with tears.

"Sad for her," he agreed, "but sadder still for Scotland. Almost a dozen different nobles claimed the throne, every one of them with an army to support him. Suddenly there was a danger that Scotland would be plunged into years of civil war."

"So, did they fight, all those different nobles?"

"I am getting to that. Do not run ahead of me, Marjorie."

"I am sitting behind you, Uncle!" I said, which provoked him to gales of laughter.

Under us, Grey Glennie trembled, and I could feel little shivers like worms running beneath her skin. When the horse had settled, Uncle Neil continued.

"No, they did not fight. To stop them, the council then running the country decided that they had to bring in someone from outside to judge the claims. And who did they pick as the only man who could perform such a task?"

I could not guess. "Who?"

"King Edward of England!"

The grey mare suddenly shied, stepping sideways, and I grabbed hold of Uncle Neil's belt even tighter than before.

"That is like asking the fox to guard the henhouse, Uncle."

"Indeed it is, child." He laughed again. "Indeed it bloody well is. But only a king can choose a king, or so it was thought. Now, having already conquered Wales, King Edward saw a chance to unite the whole of Britain under his own greedy rule. So, he agreed to act as judge, but only if the winner accepted him as overlord."

Now Grey Glennie was quiet again and I had time to think.

At last I said, "But Uncle, if Edward Longshanks chose the king yet was still overlord, then what did being king here really mean?"

He turned his head and looked over his shoulder at me. "You see—you have your father's mind!"

I glowed under his praise, and my cheeks felt burnished like a copper cup straight from the maker.

"So what *did* being king here really mean? Well, little Jo, most of the Scots nobles already owned lands in England, which meant they already had to pay homage to the English king."

"Like Father," I said.

He nodded. "And since none of them wanted to ruin his chance of being chosen Scotland's king, they all agreed to Edward's terms."

"Oh." I thought about that. About how money and land make men both powerful and powerless.

But Uncle Neil was not done. "So the choice boiled down to two men, your great-grandfather, head of the Bruce family— and John Balliol, who had the support of the powerful Comyns."

This part I knew. Father and the uncles had been speaking of it the night before. "Edward Longshanks chose Balliol," I said.

"Yes. Edward knew Balliol was a weak man who could be bullied into submission. In fact, we Scots called Balliol *Toom Tabard*, the empty coat. In other words, King Nobody."

"King Nobody," I repeated. "I think it would be better to be an earl's daughter than Princess Nobody."

Uncle Neil snorted and turned once more to look at me. "When Toom Tabard finally made a stand against Edward, it was too late. He was defeated and forced to give up the throne."

I beat my hands against Uncle Neil's back to show I approved. "Was that when he was sent off to France, Uncle?"

"Indeed. King Edward now openly assumed the kingship of Scotland, crushing any who opposed him, like William Wallace, who fought bravely until he was captured and murdered."

I shuddered. I knew something about William Wallace, the famous Braveheart. Tall and handsome and our very own hero. Everyone in Scotland knew *that* name. And they knew as well that less than a year earlier he had been hanged, then cut down and his body sliced open, and . . . I shivered. What if Father suffered the same fate? Or the uncles? I began to shake uncontrollably and put my arms around Uncle Neil.

"So, now there is no one left to lead the Scottish cause," Uncle Neil concluded.

"Except Father," I whispered.

"Except your father." Uncle Neil's voice was strong.

We were out of the woods now and trotting along the open road. Ahead I could see the battlements of Castle Dumfries, and well before it the spires of Greyfriars Abbey.

Soon we passed through the outskirts of Dumfries where the Greyfriars Church stood. From up ahead I could hear a hubbub of voices shouting, yelling, even screaming.

From the way Uncle Neil stiffened in the saddle, I knew this babble was out of the ordinary. He turned to speak.

"The mob's voice is coming from the abbey," he said, worry writ large on his face. "That is where your father arranged to meet John Comyn this morning."

"What does all the shouting mean?" I must have looked stricken for he patted my hands, which were still around his waist.

"Hold on tight," he told me. "We are going to find out."

I swallowed hard and gripped his belt so tightly, the edge of the leather cut into my palms. Then he spurred his horse forward and the citizens of Dumfries had to leap out of our way as we galloped past them toward the abbey.

When we reached there, Uncle Neil reined in sharply as a crowd frantic with alarm rushed toward us, hands upraised.

"Murder! Murder!" they were yelling. "There's been murder done in the sanctuary."

And one man, with a dark cap on his head, added, "God's house has been stained with blood."

Neil leaped down.

"Father," I cried, sliding off the horse into Uncle Neil's arms.

8 ∾ DUMFRIES, SCOTLAND, FEBRUARY 1306

When I slid into Uncle Neil's arms, I thought my father dead, murdered in the cathedral by Red Comyn.

And then the man with the cap cried out, "Red Comyn has been slain on the altar steps!"

I was so relieved, I began to shake.

It was not Father, then, who was dead.

I could not cry for Comyn, that treacherous worm. But the man said nothing further. Was Father hurt, too?

"Uncle Neil?" I cried, but he was already pressing through the crowd, which parted before him like water before a ship's prow. I grabbed the tail of his tunic and he carried me along in his wake.

Once we neared the churchyard, the crowd grew thinner as if nervous about approaching too close to the center of the disturbance.

Here and there among the alders and tombstones I recognized many of my father's soldiers who had often visited Lochmaben. I did not know their names, but their familiar faces lent me some comfort.

Grey-clad monks came scurrying out of the abbey, looking for all the world like rats deserting a sinking ship.

"Father!" I whispered, too afraid to say it aloud.

Then a body of armed men, led by Uncles Edward and Alexander, marched purposefully toward the castle, crying out, "King Robert! King Robert! The people's king!"

Some folk raised a cheer as they passed while others shrank back into their doorways. Most of the soldiers waved their bonnets, shouting for their new king.

King Robert.

Then I knew he had to be alive and well.

Then suddenly there—in the middle of all the excitement— was Father, standing by the entrance to the abbey and conferring solemnly with a group of men. He was hatless, and there was a deep scarring on the breast plate of his armor. Pointing to the left, he barked out some quick orders.

For a moment I could not speak. Then his name came tumbling from my lips, unstoppable.

"Father! Father!"

In all the tumult, he heard my voice and knew it. Turning, he spotted me, and his mouth opened in surprise.

Leaving Uncle Neil, I ran up to embrace Father, but pulled up short when I saw the state of his tunic. The sleeves were splashed bright red with blood.

"Are—are you hurt?" I stammered.

He bent down and gave me a reassuring smile, but his face held no happiness. It was a look I had never seen on him before, a mix of grief, shame, anger, and something else. I might have called it hope. Or despair.

"Do not fear," he said. "The blood is not mine." Then his face darkened. "How did you get here?"

Uncle Neil came up and placed a hand on my shoulder.

"She insisted on coming, Robert, and I . . . I indulged her," he said apologetically. "I had no idea." Lost for words, he waved his hand at the chaotic scene that surrounded us.

"You *always* indulge her," Father said sharply. "And you *rarely* have an idea."

Uncle Neil flinched at his words, then grinned boyishly, that smile that always won over Father—and everyone else.

"But . . . "—Father looked back at me—"I suppose there is no harm done. Not by you at least. Not this day."

Uncle Neil shook his head in bewilderment. "Robert, what has happened? Already they are proclaiming you king."

Father took Neil's arm and drew him aside. They seemed to have forgotten I was there.

"Red Comyn is dead," Father said grimly. "We met in the abbey as arranged. I did not mention to him that I had heard he was selling me to Longshanks. Instead, I spoke of peace between us, of Scotland's freedom. He would have none of it. He accused me of treachery and dishonor. *Me!*"

Uncle Neil ground his teeth. "He is a fine one to talk of treachery!"

Or honor, I thought. I pulled my cloak around me. Even though the day was sunny, I was suddenly cold.

"Comyn began to draw his sword," Father said, "and spoke wildly of dragging me back to England. Drew his sword! What could I do? I had no choice but to pull out my dagger and strike him down." His face contorted for a moment. "May God forgive me for committing such a deed in a holy place, but it was his life or mine." He shook his head. "That he had so much blood in him . . . "

"What about his followers?" asked Uncle Neil.

"They tried to avenge him at once, of course. Old Sir Robert

Comyn struck me on the breast with his sword, but thank the Lord it was deflected by my armor. Seton cut him down where he stood, and the rest fled."

"I do not doubt you did what you had to," said Uncle Neil, putting his hand on Father's shoulder. "But now we will have the Comyns and all their allies lined up with the English against us."

Father shook the hand off. "Think you I have not considered this?"

"Of course, Robert, but—"

Father's face was grim. "That is why I have only two courses open to me," he said. "To flee Scotland. Or take the throne."

Neil grinned wolfishly. "That's nae choice."

Father nodded. "Nane indeed."

I drew in a deep breath but knew better than to interrupt.

More men gathered around, almost blocking Father from my sight. There was shouting in the back of the crowd, and someone turned too quickly, his elbow striking me in the head.

I must have cried out, for Father reached for me, and drew me close. Safe in the cage of his arms, I suddenly began to shake. He continued speaking to Uncle Neil, his voice low and urgent. "We know which castles must be secured, which towns brought under our banners. Bishops Wishart and Lamberton have already pledged the support of the church."

"I'll send messengers to our allies," Neil enthused.

Shaking his head, Father said, "No, no, Neil. For now I want you to take Marjorie back to Lochmaben. This is no place for a child. She has already been hurt. See the red mark on her forehead?" His hand smoothed my hair back from my brow. "I want her away from here before there is worse."

"I am fine, Father," I said, pulling away. "Really."

But he did not hear me. Instead he continued speaking to Uncle Neil. "See Lochmaben is well fortified, the women safe. God knows what Longshanks will do should he get his hands on them."

Uncle Neil's handsome face grew dark. "You cannot believe he'll be marching against us so soon?"

Father pulled me back, as if to keep me safe. "I cannot believe he will not. Plan for the worst, hope for the best, Neil. Besides, if he does not come himself, Longshanks has allies aplenty to do his bloody work. Comyn was not alone in his treachery. You can be certain of that."

Uncle Neil nodded.

As if musing, Father added, "The curtain wall at Lochmaben is strong. Grandfather built well." His head snapped up and he added curtly, "Send men to divert water from the loch to flood the ditches."

"Yes, Robert," Uncle Neil said.

"Edward, Alexander, and Thomas will stay here with me to secure Dumfries Castle. If we hurry, we can surprise them and send the justices back to England. It will be quite a poke in the eye for Longshanks."

Neil grinned at that.

"When all is done, we will join you."

"Take me with you, Father," I pleaded. "I want to see you capture a castle."

Father frowned and touched a finger to his tunic. "This is as much blood as I ever want you to see, Marjorie," he said. "Though I fear it will not be the last spilled this day."

9 ❧ THE THIRD DAY OF MY CAPTIVITY

It is past the midnight bell. The long tolling wakes me.

I open my eyes a crack and see moonlight running in silvery streaks down the bars of my cage.

And I see something else, too. Someone standing about ten feet away, watching me, as a hawk watches a mouse.

Without lifting my head or giving any sign that I am awake, I stare at my visitor through slotted eyes.

He is plainly dressed, an old man with a hood drawn up over his head against the cold. Old—but very tall. The tallest man I have ever seen. Almost a giant, I think, and shiver. In the tales giants eat little girls. But this is not a tale and I do not believe he is here to devour me.

The moon is full in his face and has cast his features in silver. I can make out a beard, the grey of polished steel, and a pair of sharp, intense eyes. He has broad, bony shoulders but they are hunched as though carrying a heavy weight. The soldiers who stand on either side of him, but three paces behind, look poised to catch him if he should start to fall. That would be like catching a felled tree, I suppose.

He watches me for at least a full minute, maybe more. Then he turns and walks away, the soldiers falling in step behind him. He has made no gesture nor spoken the least word, but I know who he is.

He is Longshanks. King Edward of England.

My father's enemy—and mine.

Dear Lord, I can scarce catch my breath.

King Edward, here. At the priory. At my cage.

Then it was he who has ordered me into this thing.

The English call us Scots monsters. But what of their king, who cages little girls to spite their fathers? Who hangs, draws, and quarters the heroes like Wallace who range against him?

The wee bit of breath goes out of me. Why is he here? Perhaps he plans to kill me, too.

Then I must try to be a hero and so deserve my fate.

But, oh, I am suddenly so afraid.

What is a bit of wind and some old turnips to this? For now I remember what "hanged, drawn, and quartered" really means. A prisoner is hanged until almost dead, then cut down. The nearly dead body is placed on a slab. The executioner slices open the belly and draws out the heart and liver and then cuts off the head and—dear Lord—then the body is cut into quarters.

Or so I think.

The tall figure has turned and walked away, but the threat of his presence remains.

What is a cage now, but safe housing? I love this cage. Though it keeps me in, it keeps others out as well.

Keep me here, dear Lord. And safe.

Morning creeps in under a dull sky. It is much too early to awaken.

Father said Longshanks would "cruelly use" me.

Did he mean I would be put in a cage?

Or did he fear something far worse?

Like being drawn and quartered.

The plump monk has returned. This time he lifts the flap at the foot of the cage and gestures toward the cup he left yesterday.

I slide the cup out to him and he fills it from an earthenware pitcher, then passes it back to me, along with a bowl and spoon. In the bowl is an unappetizing mixture of oatmeal and water.

Scooping a small amount onto the wooden spoon, I taste the porridge. It is cold and thick and nasty and sweet. I screw up my face.

"In Scotland they would serve this hot," I tell him. "And they would add a pinch of salt."

He picks up his pitcher, turns his back, and starts to leave.

I cannot prevent myself from calling after him. "Wait. Kind brother. Stay with me awhile!"

He continues his slow, shuffling steps away.

"Are you deaf? If so, may God forgive my asking."

There is a hitch in his step; he almost trips over his long robe.

He shrugs, shakes his head. Then he continues in his slow way to the priory. Ah! Not deaf, but not allowed to speak.

I make short work of the gruel. The English may not know how to cook oatmeal, but at least there is enough of it. It fills my belly for now.

Soon, I suppose, the peasants will return and taunt me.

Their chores done, they will have no other entertainment than the girl in the cage.

Well, let them come. I shall ignore them. They are low, common, and English. Not worthy of my attention.

Dear Lord, let me ignore them.

Or let one speak with me.

10 ❦ SCONE, SCOTLAND, MARCH 1306

For the coronation, my stepmother had the most beautiful dress made for me, the over-gown of purest green silk with an open neckline sewn with pearl sequins. The long sleeves felt like angel wings. I had slippers with silver buckles. And I wore a wreath of flowers with a long, gossamer veil trailing behind. My hair was still down over my shoulders, of course, not braided and drawn back into a bun like my aunts'.

"It is beautiful," I gasped. "I look like . . . like—"

"Like a princess," Aunt Christina finished for me, patting the colored netting on her hair. "As well you should." She and Aunt Mary, my father's sisters, were admiring their own splendid dresses in the glass.

"Robert should not have gone to such," Aunt Mary said, blushing. Almost anything made her turn red; she was shy and modest in all things.

Not so Aunt Christina. Dark where Mary was fair, loud where Mary was soft, she made a complete turn and still kept her eyes on her reflection the whole way round.

I gazed out the window at the great green lawns that swept down to a small burn. It was a lovely day for the crowning. God was smiling on Scotland, though the English were not. March can be so fickle, rain one day and sun the next. But this day the skies were clear and it was not cold.

My stepmother made an entrance then, dressed more magnificently than any of us, in cloth of gold with a brocaded bodice. As always, her hair was pulled back severely, and she had that faraway, handsome stillness about her. But she did not seem comfortable. Or happy.

"Are you all ready?" As ever her voice was brisk. "The ceremony will be starting shortly. The bishops and earls are already in their seats. We must not be late." She meant the last for me, but I was already dressed and thought her unfair. It was the aunts who were still fussing.

Stepmother led us out of the guest house where the monks of Scone Abbey had quartered us. Lifting our skirts to keep them clear of the old dead grass that was still wet from the night before, we headed toward the chapel. Soldiers stood straight as we passed and I heard Aunt Christina giggle over all the attention. As usual, Aunt Mary just turned red.

Father was standing next to Mary's and Christina's husbands. He was a head taller than they, and looked very much the lion to their lambs. When they saw us they came over, all grins, to accompany their wives into the chapel.

I felt left out, having no escort of my own, till Uncle Neil appeared at my side. He was very handsome in a blue silk doublet that matched his eyes, and a scarlet samite surcoat to his knees, that was belted with a golden chain.

"Let *me* escort the most beautiful princess of all," he offered grandly.

I gave him a little punch on the shoulder. "I am the *only* princess."

He pretended to flinch. Then he bowed to me, I curtsied back, and we linked arms.

Inside the chapel, the benches were already packed with soldiers and priests, with earls and lairds and their ladies, but places had been set aside for the royal party.

Us.

Father took his seat on a simple wooden throne by the altar, facing the congregation. Behind him was a great banner emblazoned with lions and scarlet lilies.

"The king's banner," Aunt Christina whispered to me, inclining her head toward the throne.

I thought again how tall Father looked, how regal, in his great brocaded surcoat. His eyes were clear and seemed to be seeing farther than any of us. My stepmother had trimmed his beard and hair, not letting even his manservant do the task. I think she wanted to cut out the little bits of grey that had begun to show at his temples. There was nothing she could do about the salty look of his beard.

We women had to sit behind Neil and my other uncles, so I was between Aunts Mary and Christina.

Uncle Neil turned around and dimpled at me. "Really the king should be sitting on the Stone of Destiny, but old Longshanks stole that years ago, along with our crown and the rest of the royal regalia." He made a face. "Lucky for us Bishop Wishart has come up with another set of robes and vestments for the king, *and* a new crown."

"I knew that," I said, making a face back at him before I remembered I was a princess and above such things.

The bishop came in then, looking very imposing in his long, priestly robes. The mitre he wore on his head made him taller than all those around him. Even Father.

"It should really be the Earl of Fife who places the crown on the king's head," Aunt Christina told me. "But he is being held hostage in England."

Stepmother turned around then, put her finger to her lips, and hushed us both to silence. The bishop had already taken up his position before the altar and the ceremony was beginning.

There was a lot of talk in Latin that I could not follow, and it seemed to go on and on. Eventually, though, the bishop produced a golden circlet. He raised this on high, displaying it to the whole audience, then with huge dignity set it on my father's head.

He is king! I thought. *Of all Scotland!*

I was so proud I wanted to clap and cheer, but everyone else was being quiet and respectful, especially my stepmother, so I held myself back. But inside I was shouting so loudly with joy, it was a wonder that no one could hear.

Father then made a series of vows about protecting Scotland and preserving the rights of her church and people. He was so solemn, not smiling once, though those of us watching were wreathed in smiles. When Father was finished, Uncle Neil turned on his bench and winked at me and I had to bite my lip to keep from laughing out loud.

Then one by one the nobles and churchmen stepped forward, knelt, and swore their loyalty to him, though of course we women did no such thing for it was considered that if our husbands and brothers and fathers were loyal, we would be, too.

At last Father stood, came down off the dais, and took Elizabeth by the arm. Somewhere a trumpet sounded a fanfare and we marched out of the church in a stately procession.

There was a cheer as we came into the light and we all squinted because the little chapel had been so dark and close.

Soldiers and monks were lined up on every side, part guard and part celebrators.

Tables had been set out with food and drink. I counted walnuts and chestnuts, cheeses of several kinds, as well as cooked chicken and lamb and great slabs of venison. Poached salmon sat side by side with trout, beady dead eyes staring up into the light. On one table were the *voide:* cakes of so many varieties, I could feel my stomach aching as if I had already eaten to the bursting point. The most beautiful sugar-crafted *solteties* were set amongst the food. One was a crown, the next a replica of our family banner, and the final one a full standing portrait of Father and my stepmother in the very clothes they were wearing this day.

I could not believe I could be happier than this moment. Father the best possible king for the country. And I—I was a princess!

Suddenly there was an uproar from the back of the crowd. I could not see, being too short, so I ran back up the little hillock on which the church sat.

There, coming toward us, was a troop of riders, at least a dozen in all. They were mounted not on light riding horses but on great destriers, those powerful steeds that carry knights into battle.

I put my hand up to my mouth. Had Edward Longshanks found us here in the heart of Scotland?

"Father!" I cried in warning, but my voice was drowned in the sound of swords scraping out of their sheaths.

The crowd gave way before the horses, like sparrows scattering before a cat, and spear men rushed to the fore. Their weapons formed a hedge of sharpened steel.

The uncles—none of whom had gone into the little church with swords—seemed suddenly to have them in their hands. They made a tight circle around the king and queen.

Aunts Christina and Mary spotted me on the hill and, lifting their skirts, ran to grab me by the hands. Hurriedly we backed toward the church and sanctuary. I stepped on my hem and heard it rip and gave a little cry.

The riders reined in and found themselves confronted by a wall of sharpened steel.

Undaunted, the cloaked leader jumped to the ground and strode toward Father, calling out, "Robert! Robert! You started without me."

Strange to say, the soldiers all gave way.

Then, the war leader flung back the folds of cloak, and we could all see—even from the hillside—that it was a woman. She had been riding astride! When she pulled off her bonnet, her bright red hair rolled down her back like a cascade of fire.

"I've come to see our new king *properly* crowned," she declared.

An excited buzz passed from lip to lip. Evidently everyone recognized her but me.

I tugged at Aunt Mary's skirts and hissed, "Who is that?"

"Isabel, Countess of Buchan," she replied, her entire face scarlet.

Isabel, I thought with a thrill. *The same name as my mother.*

Aunt Mary continued, "She is the sister of the Earl of Fife, so I suppose she can perform his duty for him."

"It is passing strange that she be here, though," Aunt

Christina said, pulling me down the hill as if I were a little babe on leading strings. "Her husband is one of the Comyns and a close ally of King Edward. She risks everything by coming here."

When we reached the crowd, Aunt Christina bulled us through till we were standing but a foot away from Father, and closer still to Isabel.

She was saying in a loud but lovely voice that her brother would have come to crown the king had he been able. "He is held as a ward in Longshanks's court." She fairly spit out the English king's name. "Yet if we are to be true Scots, free and brave, we need the strength of our traditions. Therefore, I have come to stand in my brother's place. I am here to crown King Robert in the ancient manner."

Father embraced her. "Isabel, having you here is worth more than a thousand men flocking to my banner."

"The men will come in time, Robert," she assured him with a grin. "But, for now, let us see you properly made king."

The Bishops of St. Andrews, Moray, and Glasgow gathered around Father, who handed his golden circlet back to the abbot of Scone. Then he knelt in the old grass in front of Isabel. The abbot passed the crown to the countess, and with solemn dignity she placed it on Father's head.

"There," Isabel said and, turning, smiled at the crowd.

Father got to his feet and a cheer went up that must have driven any lingering clouds from the sky. The sun blazed down on the scene and the pipers sent up a skirl of wild music.

"Long live the king!" That was Uncle Neil.

"Good King Robert and Scotland!" That was the other uncles.

"Hurrah!" I cried. "Hurrah!"

The soldiers echoed me with their own shouts.

And then the party began in earnest.

It was everything I could have imagined. Earls and their ladies, knights and bishops, musicians and dancers all mixing together. There were chieftains from the northern mountains wrapped in rough lengths of plaid, wealthy nobles in fur-lined pelices, ladies in fabrics that shimmered like water in the light. Drummers and pipers struck up a jig and we all started dancing with whoops of joy.

Now I could forget all the fears—and the blood.

Now I could forget my torn skirt.

I went over to one of the long tables and was about to help myself to a pastry when a hand reached over my shoulder and plucked a sweet from a serving dish. When I looked up, I saw Isabel of Buchan standing over me. She was still in her riding gear but to my eyes she looked far more magnificent than any of the other ladies in their silk and gold.

She gave me a half bow.

"Princess Marjorie," she said. "I would know that face anywhere."

"But we have not yet met," I answered, my mouth full of pastry.

"You have your mother's nose and eyes. I was introduced to her in Carrick years ago when I was younger than you are now. We laughed that we had the same name. She was very kind to me when I needed a friend. I have never forgotten her." She finished her sweet, then turned, and plucked up an oatmeal bannock, which she disposed of in two bites.

"I am half starved," she confessed. "We have had a

long, hard ride this morning. It is a good thing that I kept my husband's best horses for myself when he went off to England."

"Is your husband one of Father's enemies?" I felt bold with her.

She nodded slightly.

"Will he not be angry with you for what you have done?"

"He will if he can catch me." Isabel laughed, a gay, delighted sound. "I was married off to that fool for the sake of some land, but my first loyalty is to Scotland and my king."

I thought about that. I could not imagine anyone making her do what she did not want to do. My confusion must have shown on my face.

"Ah, I was younger then. But no one will cage me that way again." She laughed. "Now the sword's out and the scabbard has been thrown away. This is the time we will separate the true Scots from the pismires."

At that moment I knew that I would follow her anywhere just to have her laugh again.

"How can you waste time gossiping when you should be up dancing?" accused a familiar voice.

We both turned to see Uncle Neil, holding out a hand to us.

Isabel arched her left eyebrow at him. "I will not swallow a challenge like that from you, Neil Bruce." She hooked her arm around his and led him into the dance.

For a moment I was jealous. But then I thought that if Uncle Neil was going to dance with anybody, I was glad it was Isabel. So, instead, I looked around for my father. I wanted to tell him how proud I was. That he was king. That I was his daughter. When I finally caught sight of him, I was disappointed to see that my stepmother had pulled him away from the celebrations. They were talking earnestly under a tree.

I decided to grab him by the hand and pull him to the dancing ring as Isabel had done with Uncle Neil. We would show everyone how the royal family could jig and reel.

Running over to where they were standing, I realized suddenly that they had not even seen me. I stood there awkwardly, listening in to what was surely a private conversation.

"Rejoice, my dearest," Father was saying, "for you have been made queen and I am the king."

"I fear, sir," said my stepmother with downcast eyes, "that we have been made king and queen of the May, after the fashion of children in summer games. With no more authority than that."

"Why should we not enjoy ourselves like children?" Father said. "We have so much to be glad of."

She shook her head. "Barely even half of Scotland supports your cause, Robert."

"*Our* cause, my heart." He held her hands to his chest.

"Robert, listen to me. The rest of the country will join Edward when his armies march against you."

"When they come, I will be ready," Father promised.

Sighing, she said, "Husband, you are only a new-fledged eagle. Your wings are small and your beak's not yet sharp."

"Sharp enough to fight an old vulture, my love."

She shook her head. "What of the rest of us? And what of the family we might yet have together?"

"There will be time for all of that," he assured her. "After."

"I worry more about what is to come before."

Just then Father noticed me and his face lightened at once.

"Look, here's Marjorie. I do not doubt she is seeking a partner for the dance. Will you let me lead her into a reel?"

My stepmother nodded. She was never one to kick her heels in a jig.

So Father took me by the hand and we joined Isabel and Uncle Neil and the others. As we spun around, past Aunt Christina and her handsome husband, Seton, past Aunt Mary dancing with one of the earls, past soldiers reeling awkwardly and laughing at one another's missteps, I could see my stepmother still standing some distance off, that cold mountain, always watching.

Why, oh, why, I wondered, as my head spun from all the dancing, *can she not be more like Isabel?*

11 ❧ THE FOURTH DAY OF MY CAPTIVITY

The peasants did not come yesterday, but they are here today.

I do not know what kept them away. Perhaps it was the harvest. Or the soldiers. Or a message from God.

But before they can fling more than a few stones, there is something more interesting to watch. A long train of at least a dozen wagons approaches from the south with a small band of horsemen riding ahead.

My body has a sudden memory of riding in the smelly cart, and I shudder.

But no one sees. My tormentors have run off, shouting and jostling for better places to view the newcomers.

I cross myself quickly, blessing whomever has sent this new entertainment.

As the wagons rumble nearer, I can see that they are piled high with fine tables and chairs, screens and hangings, carpets and lamps. There are chests of clothes and linens, and barrels that I know have to be full of food and wine.

My stomach growls in protest.

Someone shouts, "It's the king's goods."

Someone else calls out, "Then he'll be staying here in Lanercost a good while."

A third cries: "God bless good King Edward!"
And they all cheer.

By the time the wagons roll through the gates of the priory, the crowd has lost all interest in me. They drift back to their cottages to spread the latest news.

I slump down with my back resting against the bars. Good solid bars. They keep the English mob out even as they keep me in. I will praise them until Father rescues me. Or Uncle Neil.

Thinking about that train of wagons, I realize the mob is right. Edward Longshanks must be planning to stay a long time to have brought so much with him.

But why here? Shouldn't he be marching on into Scotland at the head of his army? What keeps him on the border, in Lanercost?

As if in answer to my thoughts, I hear voices coming from the direction of the priory.

"Be careful, Your Majesty," someone says, mooing like a lovesick cow. "You are not yet steady on your feet. We should have called for your litter."

"Let go of my arm!" comes a low growl. "I can walk to the damned cage without your assistance."

The old man who watched me last night stumps over the grass toward me. This time his hood is thrown back and in the grey morning light his face looks terribly fierce, as if every one of his battles has been imprinted there. His skin is as yellow as a parchment map. He is dressed as plainly as any ordinary knight, in a loose brown tunic. It almost makes me laugh to see the skinny little servant who flutters about him. Especially since he is dressed in bright yellow with scarlet hose. Like a bird around a bull.

Two armed soldiers follow as Longshanks comes toward me. Waving the servant away, he makes a complete circle of the cage. He runs his gaze over the bars and nods to himself. I do not know why but I can guess. He seems grimly satisfied with my condition. Like a bear keeper with his tamed beast.

I stand and hold my head high. He shall not make me cringe away from him. I am a princess, after all.

At last he stops and looks at me directly.

I stare back, defiant.

He opens his mouth to speak, and his mouth is partially toothless, which makes it look like a vast cavern. I wonder if I will fall into it.

However, before he can utter a word, he is shaken by a fit of coughing. As he doubles over, his yellowed face flushed with crimson, he grabs one of the bars of the cage to support himself. The cage shakes a bit and I try not to laugh.

"Thank you, dear Lord," I mouth. In this game, whatever it is, I have won the first counter. Father and Uncle Neil would be proud.

The attendant rushes over, pulling a white cloth from his belt, and tries to swipe at the king's reddened face, but Long-shanks will not have it. He draws himself up with a deep breath and angrily brushes the attendant aside. In fact, he looks set to cuff the poor man about the ears and the man hops away to a safe distance.

Then Longshanks darts a sharp glance at me to see how I have reacted to his fit.

The fury in his face frightens me and I lower my eyes, like any beast in a cage.

One point for Longshanks.

There is a pause as he draws in a long, slow breath. He runs a finger across the cage bars, as if to show me he does not need to hang on to them any longer.

"Do you see, girl," he says in a low, ragged voice, the voice of an old man, "do you see what your father has brought you to?"

His words take me by surprise and I bite my lower lip.

He chuckles. It is not true laughter. There is no feeling of amusement in it. "Oh, yes, it is all your father's doing, as surely as if he himself turned the key in the lock."

I look up and see that his thin lips are twisted more into a grimace than a smile.

"You have made a mistake, sir, for it is you who are my jailer, not my father." My voice sounds very small and very far away, not the voice of a princess at all.

"I am your king, girl, not your jailer," Longshanks rasps. "And that is how you will address me."

I swallow hard. I can feel my legs trembling under my filthy skirts. Has he noticed? I cannot let him see that I am afraid. If only I can get control of my legs. And my voice.

"The only king I recognize . . . "—my voice falters and tries to fail me but I will not let it—"is my father, who is king of Scotland." There, I have managed it, though my beastly legs are as shaky as Cook's pudding.

Edward Longshanks' eyes flare like bonfires. He shifts to get a better view of me through the bars. "Your father is a brigand wearing a stolen crown. I will take the crown from him. And his head with it."

"No!" I gasp. "Never!"

"Think you I cannot?" Longshanks says. "I have you. His

sole heir. His flesh and blood." His voice is quiet, as a snake's voice is quiet.

"Is that why you hate me so much?" My nose has started to drizzle but I do not bring up a hand to wipe it away. "Is that why you have caged me here where your people can insult me and throw things?"

He must have noticed my running nose and the tremor in my voice. He certainly can smell me, for I am weeks from my last real bath. Indeed, he looks triumphant. He sticks his face right up to the bars.

"You are too small and insignificant for me to waste such passions on," he says. "But my people have every reason to hate you and all you stand for." He smiled slowly, showing his few uneven yellow teeth. "Count yourself lucky that you have these bars to protect you, little mistress. Otherwise my people might have killed you by now."

"If they do kill me, it will be a blessing," I say, struggling to hold back tears. "For then I would be free in God's kingdom! Not a prisoner in yours."

I turn away and cover my face with my arm and sob. I am ashamed of my sudden weakness in the face of the enemy. Through my sobs I can hear Edward and his escort walking back to the priory, their victory won.

Evening draws on. I want to settle down. I want to sleep. But my mind boils with memories.

Suddenly I recall Father saying to my stepmother that I have a useful knack for stealth.

It would be better if I had a talent for martyrdom. Or the courage of a knight. Instead, I am but a twelve-year-old girl, many miles from safety and a long way from home.

I lie down and wriggle about, trying to find a comfortable spot. The floor of the cage is as cold and unyielding as Longshanks' heart.

It is also the same yellow oak color as his face. Yellow is a fine color for wood, but not for a man. Unless, of course, that man is deathly ill.

I sit up, stunned.

Only now do I understand.

Edward Longshanks is much too ill to press on at the head of his troops. He is too sick to lead his army into battle against my father.

So he has brought me here in my father's stead to wage his war against me.

Perhaps my age will work for me, then, not against me. For he is old and sick and I am young and well.

It is all I have. But perhaps it is enough.

12 ❧ SCONE, SCOTLAND, APRIL 1306

After the coronation, I expected we would leave Scone to move into a palace.

Stirling perhaps.

Or Linlithgow.

Or even Edinburgh Castle.

I imagined a huge and splendid building with turrets, flags, and banners fluttering in the breeze, spacious halls heated by roaring fires. And lots of servants.

Instead we ended up in Sir Alexander's country estate, Weems. It was far west of Scone. Pleasant enough to look at, it was called a manor house, which sounds as if it should have been large and imposing, but it had small rooms and bare walls. The beds were cramped and the food was simple and boring. They kept cattle and pigs nearby. The smell seeped into the house on the warm spring days.

Even Lochmaben was bigger.

"Why do we remain here, Stepmother?" I asked. "If Father is king, why are we not in a castle?"

She shook her head as if disappointed with my question and took another stitch in her embroidery.

It was Uncle Neil who explained. "English garrisons still hold Stirling and Edinburgh. Until we have an army great enough to shake Longshanks' men out of our castles, those are no places for a Scottish princess." He smiled at me.

"We will be happy here," Stepmother added, though she looked anything but.

"Can we not return to Lochmaben then?" I asked, thinking of my cozy rug from Flanders and the pretty tapestry of birds and dogs that hung on the west wall.

"Lochmaben is close to England," Stepmother said. "The Borders are too dangerous for us right now."

How strange, I thought, *that months earlier Lochmaben had seemed the safest of havens. And now we did not dare return there.*

In the meantime, we saw hardly anything of Father and the uncles. They were riding the length and breadth of Scotland rallying their allies and raising money to support the cause. Getting together that "great army" of which Uncle Neil spoke.

Even he left us to help.

"Robert needs me now, and you do not," he told Stepmother and me. He kissed her hand, but he held me close before setting me down. His cheek scratched mine, but I did not complain.

I watched from the window until I could not tell his horse from a speck in the road. With his going, we were quieter. There were fewer things to laugh about.

Stepmother received daily letters from my father and read out the latest news to us. They sounded like nothing more than long lists of castles and towns, most of which I had never heard of.

"Dearest Heart," she read. "We move tonight to Methven." And again, "My Darling Wife, we are on to Dalry. Tomorrow, Mon Coeur, Tyndrum. Kiss my daughter for me."

I could not keep straight which places were for Father and which against him. Stepmother did nothing to enlighten me. She sat in her room, often staring out the window and sighing.

When I asked her directly, "Is Father going to be all right?" she put me off with, "God loves the Scots and the Irish."

"But *will* he be all right?"

She turned those winter eyes on me. "Do not grow attached to this farm."

That was all she said. I could not make it out. Only one thing was clear. More English were marching into Scotland.

I would not grow attached to what I could not love.

It was Isabel of Buchan who brought us word of Longshanks' progress as we waited at the farm. She arrived once again on one of her husband's warhorses. This time she was escorted only by a single man. The rest of her men—and her horses—she had given to Father for his army.

Isabel dashed into my stepmother's room, unannounced, her hair looking as if it had been combed by crows. We were there doing our embroidery. Or, rather, I was undoing my embroidery.

"Isabel!" I cried, leaping up to embrace her.

She had no time for me, turning instead to my stepmother.

"Elizabeth, news has come that King Edward's son is leading his own army against Robert's territories on the other side of Scotland." She tucked a strand of unruly hair back into its braid.

My stepmother listened gravely.

"The English still control all the southeast of Scotland from Berwick to Edinburgh and the River Forth. It is from there that another of their armies is advancing under the Earl of Pembroke."

"And Lochmaben?" I asked in a throaty whisper.

Only then did Isabel turn to me. "Alas, child, right in their path. I am sorry."

"Will Maggie be safe?"

Isabel looked at my stepmother. "Maggie?"

My stepmother did not answer her. Indeed, it was as if I were no longer in the room. The two women seemed to speak coded messages back and forth. They knew so much about the war's progress and I so little.

In that very moment, I resolved that I would learn. So I leaned forward and listened carefully to everything they said. What I did not understand, I would find out after.

"King Edward has moved quickly," my stepmother suddenly said. "Typical of him." It only then occurred to me that—like my father—she probably knew Edward Longshanks well.

How strange it must be, I thought, *to have someone you know trying to destroy you.*

And then I remembered Father's face after his fight with Red Comyn. How it had held a combination of grief, shame, and anger. I wondered if power always makes enemies of friends.

"There is worse," Isabel added solemnly. "They have raised the dragon."

I couldn't think what she meant. Surely Longshanks had not sent an actual dragon against us, with huge wings and fiery breath. I was old enough to know such things did not exist outside of the ballads and nursery tales.

"What does that mean—raising the dragon?" I asked.

They both looked at me as though suddenly remembering I was there.

Isabel deferred to my stepmother with a swift glance. Stepmother fingered her cheek for a moment. I think she was wondering whether I was old enough to understand.

"I am nearly twelve," I said. "Almost a woman."

At last, giving a huge sigh, she said, "It means that their army flies the dragon banner as a sign that they will give no quarter." She looked up to the ceiling as if seeking help there. "There will be no mercy shown to any who stand against their king. They will kill, burn, destroy until all resistance is crushed."

"Oh." My voice was small. I thought of Father, in the dragon's way. And the uncles.

"You do not seem surprised, Elizabeth," said Isabel.

Stepmother shook her head. "It is what I feared. What we *all* should have feared," she replied. "But now that the worst has come, we must stand against it and not be afraid."

"I am not afraid," I said. I put my hand on hers.

"I never thought a daughter of Robert de Brus would be," she said, and smiled down at me.

In the weeks that followed, Isabel was my consolation. While my stepmother and the aunts seemed to make endless embroideries and simply wait at the farm for news, Isabel took me out riding. There, surrounded by deep, secret woods, she told me stories of Scotland's ancient kings in their great halls, of goblins and kelpies and brave heroes with magic swords. She taught me the old songs of honor. She instructed me in the movements of this war. We became like sisters of an age, though she was ten years my senior. I was grateful for every moment she gave to me.

But like Father in simpler days, Isabel was gone much of the time, visiting her other friends and kin, encouraging everyone to put his faith in my father. I missed her dreadfully when she was away. Nothing was the same without her.

One day when Isabel was gone, my stepmother tasked me for moping around as if someone had stolen my favorite toy.

"You are acting like a spoiled child," she said.

"I do not want to be here," I told her flatly. "We should be fighting the war with Father. Or ruling from a palace like a real queen and princess."

"Wherever a queen or princess makes her home, however humble it may be, there is her palace," she told me.

"That is a stupid answer," I said. I ran off to a corner of the courtyard. There I took comfort in all the times my stepmother had been wrong, counting them up as if on a tally. I did this because I suspected in this one thing Stepmother had been right, and I did not want to admit it. I asked myself if Isabel would have answered as I had, and knew she would not.

"The only thing stupid here," I told myself, "is me." But I could not bring myself to apologize.

I was still angry with myself, and mad with worry about Father, when Isabel returned. As soon as I heard she was back, I sought her out.

She looked at me as if I were some sort of wild animal. "You have not been helpful to Elizabeth," she said, scolding me as if I were a child.

"This is not a war for you to side against me," I said.

"This *is* a war, and we are all to side together," she told me.

I sulked the rest of the day and would not speak to anyone,

so I was in the courtyard once again when a messenger arrived. His horse was lathered from a desperate ride, and he dismounted hastily, not even bothering to cool the poor beast down.

Forgetting my anger, eager only to hear what he had to report, I followed the messenger up the stairs to Elizabeth's chamber. There I stood, like a servant, listening at the door.

He gave no more preamble than, "My queen," and knelt before her. She waved him up with a quick hand.

"No niceties. Just tell me," she said. The aunts and Isabel, who were with her, leaned forward eagerly to hear what he had to say. Their skirts were spread about them like scallop shells.

"Perth is captured. Bishop Lamberton and the Bishop of Glasgow have been taken prisoner," the messenger said. "Only the fact that they are men of God has saved them from being hanged."

My jaw must have dropped. In some ways this was the first time the war seemed real to me. I remembered those two good men as I had last seen them, at the coronation, their faces aglow. Lamberton had merely tapped his foot to the music, but the Bishop of Glasgow had joined in the dance. *Taken prisoner?* I tried to picture them in a dungeon and failed.

The messenger was sent down to the kitchen for a hot meal. But the women kept speaking of what they had heard, for once their embroideries set aside. I came in from the door and sat down at their feet and listened.

"What does it mean?" Aunt Christina asked of no one, of the very walls.

Isabel paced, for she could never be still. Even when eating, she fiddled with her food. "Now that the English have got

Perth, Robert will *have* to lead his men there to confront them," she said. "Either that, or leave the road open for them to march straight north into the rest of Scotland."

My stepmother's hands wrangled together. "Is that a good idea, Isabel?"

Her voice was full of worry, but I could not help being excited by the news. If the English were this close, then Father would be fighting on his own ground. Scottish soil would lend him great strength. Surely we would now defeat the English and drive them back across the borders.

Isabel ignored Elizabeth's question, and looked up, cheeks oddly burnished. "I must join him," she said briskly, turning to face my stepmother. "I will have my horse prepared at once."

"Do not be silly, Isabel. You are a woman. There is nothing you can do in a battle," Aunt Mary told her.

"I may not be able to fight," Isabel retorted, "but I *can* tend the wounded." She pushed a stray curl back into its braid.

Suddenly I could be silent no longer. I ran up to her and grabbed her by the skirts, turning her around.

"Let me come with you, Isabel," I begged. "I can nurse the wounded, too."

Isabel looked horrified and my stepmother snorted. "You see what you have started? Do not begin what cannot be undone."

Isabel pushed me away. "No, no, Marjorie—you and the other royal ladies must remain here out of harm's way. Your father would take my head otherwise."

I was astonished by the alarm in her eyes.

"Why should he do that?" I asked.

Isabel shook her head and glared at my stepmother. "Has no one told the child? She has a right to know."

The aunts looked at one another, like chickens facing the knife.

My stepmother glared back at Isabel, then turned to me. "Marjorie, King Edward has declared all of your father's womenfolk to be outlaws. That means men may rob, assault, or murder any of us—without fear of punishment."

"Then Longshanks has raised the dragon against *us* as well," I exclaimed, feeling proud rather than afraid.

"*That* is the reality of this war," said my stepmother.

Isabel hurried off to the stables. She no longer allowed anyone to saddle her horse but kept that duty for her own. I suspected it was to keep her hands busy, for Sir Alexander had plenty of servants at the mansion to do such tasks.

I sneaked out after her. The stables were cool and musty-smelling, and quite dark in the fading April afternoon. She went to the stall where her great warhorse was kept, one of the large corner boxes. She did not see me, for I kept to the shadows until she had taken the horse into the courtyard to saddle and mount him.

In spite of what she had said in Elizabeth's room, I thought I might still persuade her to take me along. After all, I was good at persuading. Had I not gotten Uncle Neil to take me to Dumfries? And if Isabel brought me along, I could be at my father's side. None could stand against us if we were together.

I went right up to Isabel as she was adjusting the horse's girth. Her hair stuck out of its braiding, like tufts of red straw.

"Let me come," I pleaded. "I will follow your orders and be

very good and brave. You cannot just leave me here on this smelly farm when there is a whole kingdom in danger."

Isabel looked down with a hint of sympathy in her eyes. "Your duty is here," she said. "Your mother and your aunts will need you in the days to come."

"Elizabeth is *not* my mother," I retorted sullenly.

Isabel raised a disapproving eyebrow at me. "Then remember she is your queen," she said sharply.

The hardness in her voice hurt me more than a slap on the cheek. I felt my lip quiver as I stepped back and watched her mount up and, without another word, ride off into the distance.

13 ❧ THE FIFTH DAY OF MY CAPTIVITY

This night, crouched like a newborn, I dream of a wild country of steep hills and thick, impenetrable forests. It is a place like my beloved Scotland, where Father is fighting for freedom.

A voice, low and furtive, comes past the trees. I do not recognize it. It is full of strange vowels and very English. There is another voice, now. And someone sniggers. Then a scuffling sound, like claws scraping across a wooden floor.

A wooden floor!

I understand now that these sounds come from the waking world, and I try to shake myself from my dream. The forests and hills begin to sweep around me. They try to overwhelm me. I fight my way into consciousness.

I wake, still in my cage.

And there on the floor—only inches from my face—is the biggest rat I have ever seen.

I leap to my feet with a yelp and back frantically away, windmilling my arms to keep my balance. I knock over the bucket and fall against the curtain, pulling one side loose.

The rat's long nose twitches and its snakelike tail whips from side to side. It clicks its small, sharp teeth.

I have heard that babies have sometimes been killed by rats. Even older people can die of their bite.

I stamp my foot and cry out, but the rat does not run away.

Then the sniggering that had entered my dream erupts into full blown laughter behind me, where the curtain is down.

I turn and see two boys from the village standing some distance off. They are holding their stomachs as if more laughter might leak out and drown us all.

Now it comes clear. The boys have brought the rat here and released it into the cage to fright me.

Before I can shout at them, the rat darts forward, brushing against my skirts. With a scream I throw myself back against the bars while the rat snuffles around the edge of the bucket.

Then I calm myself. This is one small battle I can win. I reached down carefully with my right hand, waiting until the rat is well inside the bucket.

With a single scoop of my hand, I pick up the bucket and— screaming, "Out! Out!"—I toss the rat and my slops through the bars of the cage as far as they can go.

Have I hit the boys? I do not know. I hope so. They curse wildly, words I have never heard before.

The rat vanishes in the dark.

The boys vanish, too.

Then I hear rapid footfalls approaching. A sentry—one of Longshanks' soldiers—hurries to see what the noise is about.

So—it is the sentry, and not my scream, that has made the boys run off.

"There was a rat here!" I tell him. "Some boys brought a rat."

The soldier says nothing. He does not even look at me. Instead, he just shrugs, turns around, and marches back to his position at the priory gate.

As for me, I lie back down. To sleep if not to dream. I have discovered that if I curl up, knees to chin, on the floor of the privy area, the sackcloth drapes keep out the worst of the wind. I imagine the soldier at the gate envies me this small comfort on such an October night.

14   THE SIXTH DAY OF MY CAPTIVITY

In the morning when the monk brings me my meager breakfast, I try to tell him what has happened in the night.

"There was a rat," I say. "Boys from the village brought it to scare me, but I chased it off. And them." It is an exaggeration, not a lie.

He goes silently about his duties but looks at the torn curtain and scolds me with a shake of his head.

"How would you feel if somebody let a rat loose in your cell tonight, brother?" I ask.

He does not even have the grace to acknowledge me.

"A rat," I repeat. "It was horrible." I shiver extravagantly.

Without even so much as a shoulder shrug, he leaves.

I realize then that—with the exception of Edward Longshanks—I have no one but God to talk to.

Unlike Longshanks, God must surely listen.

So I do what I should have done all along. I talk to God.

Dear Lord, I say, please bring Father and Uncle Neil to my rescue. Shatter Longshanks' army. Pike the English soldiers' heads on our castle walls. At least bring the priory walls crashing down on these coldhearted monks.

But God does not answer either. The priory's sturdy walls do not fall. They do not even tremble.

And Father is not here.

Not yet anyway.

The day wears wearily on and I have not caught so much as a glimpse of Longshanks since we first spoke. I assume he has been too ill to come outside again.

Having no one to talk to, not even God, I have decided to talk to myself. Or at least to sing in French, lest I give the impression that I have lost my wits and thus comfort the enemy.

"Quel dommage," I sing. Then remembering Uncle Neil's description of old Balliol, I add "Mon Doo, mon-sewer" over and over as a kind of refrain.

Three peasant girls swagger by in threadbare smocks, giggling and poking one another. They are suddenly curious about my singing and come close enough to hear the words of the song, which they clearly do not understand.

One sticks her face right up to the bars of the cage. Her face is smudged and there is dirt under her fingernails. "Is it true that yer a princess?"

"Yes, it is true," I tell her, grateful for the conversation. I keep my voice low, pleasant. "For seven months now. Since my father was crowned."

"But yer all thin and dirty." Her nose wrinkles with doubt.

I look down at my own fingernails. They are as dirty as hers. Dirtier even. I touch my hair. It is already quite matted.

I try a smile. "I would be clean if someone would give me water to wash with."

She shrugs. "There's water in the well." However, she does not offer to get me any.

"I would not be so thin," I tell her, "if I had more to eat."

"I wish I had more food, mysel'," she says, running her hands over her ribs.

For a moment I gog at her. What she said sets a fire in my brain. Put a princess in a cage, I think, and in mere days she is like a peasant: dirty, hungry, horrible. Put a peasant on a throne and . . . but my mind will not go there.

Before I can say more, one of the soldiers runs down from the priory, shouting, "No one is to converse with the prisoner!"

The girls exit hastily, leaving me more alone than before. Still, it is enough to remind me that conversations can exist.

I think I shall make up a song about it. To an old Gaelic tune.

Come pretty girl, tell me true,
Am I as thin and dirty as you?
Am I . . .

I sit on the floor of my cage and sing my song over and over into the waning light. My voice cracks on a high note. The shadow of the bars fall across my lap.

Come pretty girl, tell me true,
Am I as thin and dirty as you?
Am I . . .

Suddenly I think about Father. What would he say, finding me in this filthy condition? Then I realize that he would be happy simply finding me at all.

"Your voice is weaker." It is Edward Longshanks.

He seems stronger than before, walking more steadily. When I look more closely, though, I see he is limping slightly.

Today his attendant is in a green tunic, red hose. The man stays a few paces behind him, but still looks poised to rush to his master's aid. Half a dozen soldiers are spaced out across the ground before the priory but they, too, keep well back.

Clearly Longshanks wants to talk in private.

He pats the cage as if it is an obedient dog and repeats himself. "A few days of this has taken the edge off your tongue."

"I have not had much use for my tongue," I reply. I make my reply sharp but it is an effort. "You will let no one speak to me."

"Then talk to me, if you will."

"What . . . ?" My voice stumbles. "What shall we talk about?" I do not think he wants to discuss the weather or the dirty peasantry.

"Tell me where you think your father is hiding," he says, his voice snapping shut at the end, like a trap.

"If he is hiding, it will not be for long." Father is not one to hide and we both know it. "And if I knew, I would not tell." But I wish I knew anyway.

His lip curls. "Oh, he is hiding all right. People have started calling him King Hob, the goblin king who haunts the woodlands and dares not show his face by daylight."

"King Hob," I say, in such a way that he hears it as equal to his own kingship.

"So much is his kingdom shrunk," Longshanks tells me and laughs dryly at his own weak joke.

I do not laugh with him. "Is a kingdom's size all that matters? Shame, sir. Shame." I am surprised at my sudden boldness.

Longshanks is surprised, too. "I thought you wanted someone to talk to."

I take a deep breath. "Then tell me something I want to hear."

"Which is?"

Before I can stop myself, I ask. "Tell me what you have done with Isabel and the others. Where is my . . . ?" I notice his hawk eyes watching me. It suddenly occurs to me that I should choose my words carefully. He will be looking for new ways to hurt me. I take a deep breath, then say with care, "Where is Elizabeth, the queen?"

His face wrinkles at the word "queen." In fact he looks arrow-shot. I feel I have scored a hit off him.

"Elizabeth Bruce, your father's wife," he says pointedly, "is under guard in a manor house at Burstwick. No one is to speak to her except the two crones who bring her meals. For the sake of her father, the Earl of Ulster, I have been lenient with her. God willing, she may yet see how she has been led astray, and so denounce her upstart husband."

My fingers curl around the bars. Too late I see my knuckles have gone white. Too late, I cry out, "Never!" For my stepmother is as constant as the earth.

Longshanks carries on as if I have not spoken. "Christina Bruce is already a widow, her husband having been executed after your father's defeat at Methven."

I startle. "Not good Seton!" I feel tears pool in my eyes but Longshanks ignores my outburst and continues.

"She is confined to the nunnery of Sixhills in Lincolnshire where she can nurse her grief in solitude."

I feel the pain of this beneath my breastbone, and say in a whisper, "What of my other aunt, Mary?"

He smiles. It is not a pleasant smile, for he is missing too many teeth. "We must keep something back to talk about to-morrow." He turns to leave.

Perhaps he is waiting for me to beg. But I am too numb to ask anything more. I am thinking of my stepmother in the manor house in the care of two crones. I am thinking of poor Aunt Christina. And then I am remembering her dancing with her handsome husband on the lawn at Scone, her hair come loose of its careful braiding.

As soon as Longshanks leaves me, I am certain I will cry.

But not before then.

Not so he can see.

15 ❧ SCONE, SCOTLAND, JUNE 1306

veryone was so tense over the next few days it was like living in a warren of rabbits on the edge of a fox's hole. Aunts Mary and Christina could not keep still, but were constantly finding things to weave, sew, cook, or mend.

I tried to be like Isabel, going about outdoors. Yet all I did was worry Sir Alexander's household for I insisted on riding far out, hawking till the poor hobby I was flying sat on a branch of an ancient pine and refused to come down to my glove.

Only my stepmother remained calm.

Then one afternoon, late in the week—with Isabel once again among us—a knight came galloping up to the house, his black destrier puffing and sweating. Leaping from the saddle, he threw the reins to a surprised groom and marched inside.

As we gathered in the hall to greet him—stepmother insisted on such manners—he pulled off his helmet to reveal the handsome face beneath hair matted with sweat.

"Uncle Neil!" I cried, leaping into his arms. He held me tight against his vest of chain mail.

"Little Jo, how I have missed you." He nuzzled me like a child.

His cheeks had not been shaved in days. His clothes were

disordered and spattered with blood. Many of the links on his chain mail had been broken and I noticed that the left sleeve of his shirt was torn.

"Neil," Stepmother said, "there is blood on your arm."

He put me down, and glanced at the offending arm, then shrugged as if it did not matter.

I looked carefully. I could see without a doubt that it was his own blood and shuddered.

"What . . ." I whispered, "what of Father?"

"Yes," Isabel put in, "what of Robert?"

He paused a second to draw a breath and collect himself. Then addressing my stepmother alone, he said, "Madam, you must gather your things together and have horses brought out at once."

"This moment?" She almost looked amused.

"We must get away. Now."

"But, Neil, what has happened?" Aunt Christina asked, concern for her brother's wound less than her concern for the cause.

Neil raised a hand, almost as if warding off a blow. "What has happened?" His usual smile was gone, his face looked poached, like an egg on a griddle, his eyes watery. "What has *not* happened."

We waited. It was as if none of us could breathe.

Then Uncle Neil continued, "The enemy took us by surprise near Perth, my dears. Our army was driven from the field. We have taken to the hills and the English are in hot pursuit. They could be *here* in a few hours."

"Then we still have time to see what you have done to yourself," said my stepmother, reaching out for his wounded arm.

Neil shrank back. "It was an English spear that did that, madam, and it can wait. We have to go. Now."

"And have you bleed to death on the way?" asked my stepmother calmly. "Whose purpose would that serve?"

It was a battle of wills, which Uncle Neil had never been able to win with any of the women of the family.

Stepmother sat him down on a stool and ripped the remains of his sleeve away from the wound. She frowned familiarly at the torn flesh as if she and it were of long acquaintance.

Without looking up, she said, "Marjorie, fetch a clean bowl of water and a linen cloth."

I hurried to obey her, realizing that she had spoken like a queen and I was—as Isabel once reminded me—bound to be loyal to her. Indeed I was. I ran upstairs at once to the closest bedchamber and fetched basin, jug, and cloth.

"Here," I said. "I can go for more if need be."

"No, Marjorie," she said, "stay and keep your uncle amused while I wash and bandage his wound."

She began by laving the wound with the water from the jug and catching the spillage in the basin. But it was Uncle Neil who did the amusing. He spun out the entire story of the lost battle with much vigor and too much enthusiasm for the lost cause.

"Our king," he said, his voice suddenly drawn into a storytelling hush, "planted the army before the walls of Perth and challenged the English to come out and fight us. Their leader, Pembroke, a man of infinite belly and no honor, sent word that since the day was almost done, he would meet us in battle in the morning. So we withdrew to the woods of Methven and made camp there. But while we prepared our supper and took our rest, Pembroke marched his army out and attacked us."

Stepmother sighed and shook her head. "Robert should never have taken him at his word."

Standing with her hand on Uncle Neil's good shoulder, Isabel said what I was thinking. "Robert is a man of honor and expects all to be the same."

My stepmother made a rude sound with her lips. "These are the *English* we are fighting."

I smiled to myself. Not *at* my stepmother, but in admiration of her spirit. Isabel laughed out loud.

"It was a bloody business," Neil went on, as if he were still on the battlefield. "Their knights and spear men upon us even as we reached for our weapons. We had no chance to form a battle line. Each man had to make his stand as best he could."

"And Father?" I asked fearfully.

"He is safe, little Jo, but not because of any caution on his part. He was in the very thick of the fighting, and unhorsed Pembroke himself, though he did not manage to kill the man for his treachery."

"More is the pity," Aunt Mary whispered, then put her hand up over her mouth.

"Three times Robert had his horse slain under him and three times he took a fresh mount."

Without realizing it, I clapped three times. Aunt Christina reached over and held my hand in a grip so strong, she almost broke the small bones.

But Neil was in full cry now. "Robert's courage inspired our troops to fight bravely, and so we did, the blood flowing so freely on the ground it made rivulets."

"Neil!" my stepmother said, reminding him in that one word of the ladies present.

He nodded absently but continued on grimly. "Gradually we were pushed back and back until our army broke apart."

"How bad is it?" Stepmother asked in a matter-of-fact tone as she pulled the bandage tight around his arm.

Neil winced. "Many were killed. Some of our noblest men were taken prisoner. I fear for their fates."

"But are not captured knights held for ransom?" I blurted out.

"Remember the dragon," Isabel said softly.

And then I remembered Longshanks' dragon. That meant his soldiers would show no mercy. Not to men or women or children. In my head I could see the beast already, charging north to gobble up Father and all our dreams in its fiery maw.

Once his arm was bandaged, Uncle Neil hurried us all outside and we mounted up. He carried me on his great horse and we rode ahead of everyone else. I held on around his waist, my face against his back.

I could not help enjoying the ride, even though I could imagine the blood on his chain mail coating my cheek and hands. Isabel was close behind on her own powerful charger, with the aunts and my stepmother and their several attendants ranging farther toward the rear with the pack horses.

At the beginning it was exciting enough. The furious pounding of hooves down the rutted road, the wind whipping my skirts, the feel of the steel links of Uncle Neil's armor beneath my cheek. But Uncle, lost in his own bloody thoughts, did not speak to me as we rode. After a while, the ride lost its excitement and became merely tiring. My bones began to ache, starting with the small of my back and soon extending down my legs. Once the sun began to sink, I grew sleepy.

I knew the dragon would invade my dreams.

Suddenly Uncle Neil stiffened and rose up slightly in the saddle as if spying something. I shook myself awake to see what he was seeing. Up ahead through the thick trees was a yellow glimmer of campfires. Suddenly I could smell the peaty smoke.

For a moment I roused.

A pair of bowmen appeared from the shadows as if from nowhere. Their bows were drawn and ready, but when they recognized Uncle Neil they grinned broadly and let us pass.

We traveled a hundred yards deeper into the forest till we reached the camp. Uncle Neil lowered me to the ground with his one good arm, then dismounted himself to give my stepmother a hand down. I straightened my skirts, which seemed oddly damp and clinging.

Isabel leaped off her horse on her own and turned to help the aunts, and when we were all clustered together, the men around us set up a cheer.

My stepmother inclined her head to one side and then another, nodding to acknowledge all the cheering men. Isabel and Neil waved, and the aunts perked up at the soldiers' unreserved greeting.

"Hurrah to all of you," I cried. And then, when I spotted some faces I knew—men who had come often to our keep at Lochmaben—I clapped for them. Then I cheered as heartily for them as they had me.

Uncle Neil gave my stepmother his arm and they walked through the crowd of men.

For the first time I thought how like a queen she looked, shoulders back and head high, the tiredness banished from her face. Unlike the rest of us, her hair was still in place, as if the wind from our ride had not dared dislodge a single strand.

"Hail, Elizabeth," I whispered, "queen of Scotland." I understood for the first time that she was truly a match for my father.

Just then I spotted Father walking toward us with the light of a blazing fire silhouetting his broad shoulders and striking flashes of gold from his mail shirt. His hair was a crow's wing, dark and feathering in the wind, but still familiar. Yet there was something different about him, too, as if battle had sharpened him like a blade to a keen edge. Battle—and something else, some sorrow I could not name.

I wanted to run into his arms, but I knew instinctively that I was—in this place and this time—only a princess. So I let him embrace his queen first. When his eyes met mine at last, I dropped him a deep curtsy.

"My lord, King Robert de Brus," I said.

He laughed, the skin crinkling up around his eyes. " 'Father' will do when we are alone, Marjorie." He drew me up and kissed me heartily on both cheeks, then for a moment held me to his chest. I could breathe the same breaths with him, long and slow and shuddering.

When he put me down again, the others joined us. He greeted them all with such extravagant hugs and kisses, I began to appreciate the danger we must have been in.

"We are safe enough here for the night," Father said, "but we must be off with the dawn. The English are fanning out from Perth like spilled ink spreading across a sheet of parchment." His face was a familiar map, but there were new crevices and cracks in it.

"Where are we to go?" my stepmother asked. Her voice was

so calm and practical, she might have been inquiring whether the weekly supply of flour had been delivered from the mill.

"West," my father said. "I have many supporters there and we can take refuge among the islands until I have mustered enough men to retake the mainland."

She nodded briskly. "Then we had best eat supper and sleep while we can." Almost at once she began issuing orders, waving her hands at the soldiers. They hurried to obey her as if they had been trained from birth to jump at the sound of her voice.

Father and Uncle Neil retired to a secluded spot beneath a stand of tall alders to confer with some of the men. I was just wondering if I could sneak close enough to hear what they were saying when there was a tap on my shoulder.

"Come," Isabel said. She wrapped her long braid about my wrist as if binding me to her. "Help me get the sleeping rolls and blankets down off the pack horses." She walked away, saying over her shoulder, "There is enough work for everyone this night and the soldiers have better things to do than to wait upon us."

Supper was a thin vegetable stew, the best that could be provided under the circumstances. I knew better than to complain.

Tired as I was, getting to sleep was hard. Even with a sleeping roll under me I was aware of every lump on the ground. I was still struggling to doze off while weary soldiers snored all around me. Too late I started to appreciate the comforts of the pig farm we had left behind.

In the morning I was roused by Aunt Christina to find everyone else already on the move.

"What about breakfast?" I asked, stretching my arms and yawning.

"Slugabed, you have missed the porridge. You will be eating in the saddle," said Isabel as she passed by with a bundle under her arm.

"If at all," Aunt Christina added ruefully. "At least let us get some water to wash the taste of morning out of our mouths."

I had assumed that I would be riding with Uncle Neil again, which would have been some small compensation for another long day on the road. But he had already been sent ahead to scout the way for obstacles and for any sign of the enemy.

Instead Elizabeth sought me out and told me I would be traveling with her. The queen of the night before was gone. In her place was my stepmother with her winter eyes and thin lips. She did not look pleased with my long sleep.

"I know how to ride," I said. "And well, too. Why can I not have a horse of my own?"

She pursed her lips in annoyance. "Mounts are too scarce for that," she said. "We are all doubling up, Marjorie. Gather your things and follow me."

As she turned to lead me to her horse, Isabel came trotting by, her great horse snorting as if it were expecting to charge into battle.

Why should I not ride with her? I thought to myself. But before I could ask, she was gone into the woods.

"Come along!" my stepmother called. "We can not hold up everyone for you."

Why not? I thought sourly. *I am a princess, after all.* But I knew better than to say that aloud.

For the next few weeks I seemed to be constantly in the saddle, clinging to my stepmother's skirts like a young child. The leather saddle and the horse's rough hide constantly chafed my bottom and thighs. My arms and legs grew so stiff, I could hardly move them when we stopped to camp. Yet I knew I was better off than the simple soldiers who had to trudge along on foot with their spears over their shoulders and their few belongings strapped to their backs.

We ate soldiers' rations with them: dry oatcakes and water. Only rarely was an evening hunt successful enough to bring a hare to the pot, though it was high summer and the game should have been plentiful.

Surely my stepmother felt the same aches as the rest of us, but she seemed to blossom under the hard conditions while Aunt Mary and Aunt Christina and I wilted. Our dirty faces gave us a hardened look, but Elizabeth's seemed to emphasize her strong cheekbones. We grew cranky, while Elizabeth mothered us all.

As for Isabel, she sat around the fire with the common soldiers. The firelight was no redder than her hair or cheeks. She traded stories with the men or played at counters, laughing whether she won or lost with a high, delighted ripple of sound. Much as I wanted to join her, I had little inclination to move from the warm comfort of the aunts, or Elizabeth, who let me drowse with my head in her lap.

In the third week, by way of keeping myself alert in the saddle, I tried to figure out how many men Father had in his army. As far as I knew, all that were left after the disaster at Perth were here, in our small encampment. I counted and recounted but could not make the tally come out to more than two hundred.

That seemed hardly enough to win a kingdom.

Besides, the men were all unwashed, exhausted, and angry. They marched about in small groups under their lairds' banners, or boiled in small groups, muttering to one another whenever their captains rode ahead to confer with Father.

I was certain they were brave and loyal men, but I knew that they were more farmers than soldiers, brought from their farms to fight for their king. So Isabel told me, and she had no reason to lie. Besides, if I could count, so could they. Soon they would want to be back at their own homes, gathering the harvest. How much of an army would we have then?

I tried to think of that: an army of uncles, a laird or two, Isabel tending their wounds. The English would laugh at such a band.

Dear God, I had prayed fervently, *send us more men. Soldiers this time.*

We wound our way along thickly forested hillsides, detouring around the many pools and crags that blocked our way. Even when it rained, we did not take shelter but pressed on as if the devil himself were nipping at our heels.

As indeed he was.

We were heading toward a place called Strathfillan, or so I heard several of the soldiers say. I had no idea where that was, but I hoped it was a place where we would find beds and a hot meal of lamb or venison.

I swore to myself: *If ever I am free of this endless travel, I will never eat oatmeal or vegetable broth again.*

Sometimes Elizabeth noticed how tired I was, and sang a song to cheer me up. Her voice was light and high, without much body to it, and the songs she sang were usually some nonsense about a cuckoo welcoming the spring or a lover and his lass. But I appreciated the effort and tried to sing back one of my French songs, or one of Maggie's Gaelic tunes.

Once when we rested the horse and let the foot soldiers catch up, I said to her in a kind of dreamy voice, "This is not how it was supposed to be."

She tilted her head to the right, almost but not quite looking over her shoulder. "What do you mean, child?"

I sighed then, for I felt more like an old woman than a child, every bone aching and the skin on my thighs blistered and sore. "I mean, Father was supposed to win the battles, drive the English away, and rule Scotland in peace."

"And so he shall," she told me, her lips smiling but her eyes still frosted over with winter. "In God's own time. Not yours or Robert's or mine."

16 ※ THE SEVENTH DAY OF MY CAPTIVITY

I wait all morning to hear about what has happened to my aunts and Isabel. My mind wraps around Seton's death like an old horse blanket. I stink of fear. Anyone coming past the cage will be able to smell it. For once I am glad I am alone.

The October sun, usually so weak, beats down on me. I wait long into the heat of the afternoon, afraid of the dead, of the dying. Wanting news and not wanting it.

I comb my matted hair with dirty fingers. I have been biting my nails. All I have left is one thumbnail that is not down to the quick. At least this way no one can see how much filth lies under them.

Longshanks has planned this well, that wily old soldier. He knows he is making me suffer.

He knows that if I rely on him, I am in his debt. If I am in his debt, how must I repay him?

I count the reasons I should stay on his good side: For food and drinking water. For protection. And for news.

Then suddenly I wonder: Does he tell me the truth? Does he have any reason to lie? He says my stepmother is captured, that Aunt Christina is walled up in a nunnery, that her dear husband, Christopher Seton, is dead. That Father is running for his life.

But is it all true?

Is any of it true?

If I believe it true, then he can break me.

If I believe it false, I will live to break him.

As night closes around me, he comes again, like a shadow, without his shadows.

Alone.

"Do you want to hear more?" he asks in his snake voice.

I cannot help myself. "Tell me about Aunt Mary."

He smiles. I cannot see in this evening light if he is still yellow of face, if his teeth are as yellow as before. I cannot see how sick he is.

His voice is strong, as if he feeds on my debt. "Ah, yes, Robert's sweet sister."

I force myself to be patient. The dark helps me. If I cannot see how yellow Longshanks is, he cannot see how white I am with fear. If he waits for me to beg, he will have to wait a long time.

I suspect I have more time than he. I may be in a cage with iron bars. But his cage is rotting flesh.

At last he lets a small breath escape through his teeth. Not exactly a sigh, but close. "Mary's husband still bears arms against me under your father's banner. Therefore she, too, is a traitor and has been placed in a cage at Roxburgh, where—like you—she is displayed as an example to her countrymen."

Another cage.

What kind of a man cages women and children?

I do not speak, letting the night speak for me.

He goes on, for—unlike me—he has not spent the last days in silence. Kings, I suppose, are not used to silence.

"As for Isabel, the former Countess of Buchan, her cage hangs from the walls of Berwick Castle."

This time I take a deep breath.

Isabel in a cage! I can scarcely bear it. It will be harder on Isabel than on even Mary or me. We are rabbits and she is a lion. Lions do poorly when they can not roam free.

I do not dare tell him, though. I will not give him such an easy victory. Instead I make my voice quiet, young, artless.

"Isabel of Buchan is not of our family. Why in the world should you cage her?" I know, of course, but do not let him know I know.

I can almost hear his serpent smile. "She had the temerity to place the crown upon Bruce's head," he says.

If a fist clenching can make a sound, I am certain I hear it now.

"For that," he adds, "she will stay caged until she rots."

He lies, I think. Her husband and brother will not let such a thing happen.

My father will not let such a thing happen.

God will not let such a thing happen.

I ask in my child's voice, "And what crime have I committed to deserve such a punishment?"

"You are your father's daughter. That is crime enough."

"Then I am happy to be found guilty," I say. Longshanks' curse, much to his anger, lends me strength.

This time he is the silent one.

I decide to attack with one of the few weapons I have. "Do you now have boys from the village help you in meting out your peculiar justice?"

There is an intake of breath. "What are you talking about?"

He does not know! This time I am the one to bring the news. "Two nights ago two boys released a rat into my cage."

I am certain he is raising an eyebrow. "Do not worry, Bruce's child. You will not have to put up with them much longer." There is dismissal and finality in his voice.

Does he mean the boys will be dealt with? How can he know which boys? And why should he deal harshly with his own when he has the Scots under his awful hammer?

Then my heart leaps even though my head counsels caution. Can it be that Longshanks has had enough of this game? Will I be moved to quarters in keeping with my station? Or will he simply have me killed and dump my body on the town midden?

Wait, Marjorie, I tell myself. He is playing with you. He has no future plans.

Lucky I did not speak. For he says, "Tomorrow I shall tell you more. Tonight you shall sleep troubled, wondering what the morrow will bring."

God's own time.

It was surely not ours.

Ours consisted of endless riding through forests, past filthy hamlets, up rocky hillocks, down deserted dales. Ours was porridge for breakfast, clear broth for the evening meal, cold river streams for washing, and hard ground for a bed. The only good of it was the weather, for August was mostly dry.

One day we made camp sooner than usual and, once the horses were tethered, Father's men gathered around him and followed him along a well-worn path. We women trailed behind.

I fell in beside Elizabeth but we did not talk. Indeed, a curious silence had fallen upon the whole party.

The overlacing of the trees made day into evening, late summer into later fall. An owl, certain it was night in that forest, sat above the path on a branch and glared at us with fierce eyes.

We emerged from the shelter of the trees and found ourselves in a little lea, before a plain stone tomb where a group of monks waited in two brown lines. One of them, an old abbot with a face the color and shape of a walnut, stepped forward slightly and raised his hand.

"Who comes to St. Fillan's?"

Father fell to his knees at the man's feet.

Unable to bear the mystery any longer, I whispered to Aunt Mary, "What is St. Fillan's?"

"A shrine," she whispered back. "Dedicated to the saint. He was one of Scotland's holiest men."

"If we are in such a hurry, why have we come here?"

Elizabeth silenced me with a hand on my arm. "Red Comyn's death weighs heavily upon your father," she said. "He has come here to seek forgiveness."

Forgiveness? I thought. *For killing an enemy?* But then I remembered the changes I had read in the map of his face.

As if reading my mind, Elizabeth added, "Not for killing Comyn, but for doing the deed in a holy place."

Father remained on his knees, speaking in a low private voice to the abbot, who listened closely and nodded at his words. Around us a small wind threaded its way through the trees, as if lacing them tightly together, creating a private sanctuary, a momentary haven.

At last the abbot looked up, made a sign of absolution over Father, then spoke loud enough for all to hear.

"God's forgiveness and protection is upon you, Robert. Never forget His love, nor how it can come upon you where you do not look for it. Keep that love in your heart and it will lead you to the end you seek in the fullness of God's grace."

Father put his hand up to his eyes then, as if he were weeping. I started to go to him, but Elizabeth held me firmly.

Then our whole company fell to their knees; the movement looking practiced. Elizabeth tugged me down with the rest. I banged my right knee hard, but my stubborn spirit harder.

"God's blessing be upon all of you," the abbot said, his ancient voice firm. "And may His angels guide your footsteps."

We had come to the shrine quietly, but the way back was full of chatter—about the weather, about the food, about the seasons, about the shrine, about everything but the war. The ragged column of men led the way and we women came last.

I caught up with Isabel and asked, "Is that why everything has been going wrong? Because God has been angry with Father?"

She shrugged. "Who knows why fortune favors us one day and deserts us the next? We have to bear it as best we can." She smiled at me, but some of the light had gone out of that smile.

"Surely now everything will be all right," I told her. For the first time I was leading her, rather than the other way around. "God is on our side and so is St. Fillan."

"The English pray, too," said Elizabeth, coming up behind us. "And to the same God."

Isabel laughed, though it was not hearty. She thrust a curl away from her eyes. "But God is a Scotsman now. At least here, in the Highlands."

"I hope He favors the right Scots, then," said Elizabeth. "The country we pass through next is held by MacDougall of Lorn, nephew of Red Comyn and one of your father's deadliest foes."

"It *will* be all right," I insisted, in my most grown-up voice. "The abbot promised angels will guide us."

"The abbot," Elizabeth said, smiling ruefully, "used the word *may*."

A few hard days later, heading west through the Highlands toward the islands and sanctuary, our little band looked even rougher. The men had given up even the semblance of cleaning themselves in streams. And while we women still tried to wash the dirt off each night, only Elizabeth looked as if a comb had come near her locks.

That day alone we had already gone through sun and showers and a strange hail that frightened the horses. We were riding slowly along a rocky valley. It had steep, wooded slopes rising up above us on both sides; the path was narrow and littered with rocks and boulders. Such a rough track forced the horses to pick their way carefully.

"Will we make it through before nightfall?" I asked.

"I hope so," Elizabeth replied, "because this gloomy gash will not make a pleasant campsite. There is danger all around us here."

I fell silent, and prayed to God that the horses did not go lame on the stony ground.

God's answer was a thin drizzle that gradually seeped through my cloak. I leaned my head against Elizabeth's back and shut my eyes against the discomfort.

"Must we sleep again among the hills and trees?" I said wearily. "Is there no one who will give us shelter for the night?"

"There are some," said Elizabeth, "but many more here in the Highlands are our enemies."

"They are for the English here?" I was amazed.

"They are for Comyn. Or for themselves. Besides, your father wishes to keep his movements secret to shake off any English pursuit. Why give ourselves away over a little bit of comfort?"

I nodded. Not because I agreed, but because I was too tired and miserable to argue.

Just then a gust of wind splashed a sheet of drizzle across my face and down my neck. The cold woke my anger.

"This feels like December, not August," I grumbled. "Maybe it would be better if they *did* catch us. At least they might put a roof over our heads and feed us decently."

Elizabeth's voice cracked like a whip. "Never say such a thing or you will curse us!" she snapped.

I sat up stiffly in the saddle. My throat was burning and my cheeks, too. For shame, mostly.

Above us on the rocky heights, the sodden trees dripped in sympathy with my own sunken spirits. I looked up, thinking that if God only took me at my wrong words, my life would surely be even more miserable than this.

All of a sudden I saw a movement up there, a figure darting from one tree to another.

Blinking, I looked again, but could see nothing now.

My eyes are tired and playing tricks, I thought and was about to say something to Elizabeth when there was a yell of alarm. It came from the front of our drawn-out column where Uncle Neil and Father were leading the way.

"To arms!" someone bellowed. "To arms!"

A great roar went up from the slopes above. I grabbed Elizabeth so tightly around the waist, I expect it was all she could do to breathe. Only then did I dare another look up, expecting all the while to see a fall of rocks thundering down toward us.

What I saw was far worse.

A great mob of Highland warriors had come charging out of

the trees and down the slopes. Fierce and horrible, with wild hair and long beards, they wore little more than a rough length of plaid covering their dirt-stained bodies. They looked like madmen, whooping and yelping. Each one held a long-handled axe in both hands and as soon as they reached us, they started swinging, chopping the legs out from under the horses.

Elizabeth tried to pull us away, but our horse, frightened by the yells of the Highlanders, the screams of the dying animals, reared up in a panic.

I was tossed from the saddle and tumbled head over heels, legs over shoulders, across the wet, stony ground, fetching up at last against a wall of rocks.

As the world turned end over end, all I could think was that this was all *my* fault. Surely I *had* brought a curse down upon us, just as Elizabeth had warned.

Time passed. My ears were ringing with the sound of cries, screams, the clash and clang of steel on steel, and the skirling of the bagpipes. At last I managed to get up on my hands and knees.

I shook my head groggily, then tried to look for sanctuary. All I could see was a blur of legs and horses' hooves and the fine red blur of blood as it spattered the air.

I looked down at my dress, now muddied and torn. At my hands, scraped from the fall. The blood was not mine.

Then whose? There was a horrible throbbing in my brow.

"MacDougall!" voices roared. "MacDougall!" Warriors calling out their clan name.

And then a different voice. Lighter. More insistent. "Marjorie! Marjorie!"

I knew the voice but I was too dizzy to put a name to it. Suddenly Elizabeth was kneeling beside me, brushing the hair out of my face, examining the cut at my temple.

Before I could ask her what had happened, a savage bellow made her glance up. I looked up, too. Bearing down on us was a wild Highlander, his bloody axe raised to strike.

In an instant Elizabeth had pushed me flat on the ground and thrown her body over mine.

"No!" I moaned.

There was a thud and then a high scream.

"Up quickly," someone said. "We'll fetch a horse for you."

Elizabeth stood and pulled me up by one arm. Beside her was Uncle Neil, blood dripping from his sword, the dead Highlander at his feet.

One of our soldiers brought up a horse, a dun-colored mare with a white slash down her nose.

Elizabeth clambered on and Uncle Neil boosted me up into the saddle behind her. Isabel rode up to join us as Elizabeth yanked the horse's head around to take us back the way we had come.

The battle swirled around us like a storm. Bleeding horses whinnied and kicked on the ground, wounded and dying men groaned and clutched their wounds in agony. Waves of axe men dashed against tight clusters of spears, slashing and hacking like woodcutters felling a forest. The spear men in their turn thrust their steel points forward to stab their foes.

And blood. Blood everywhere.

"Keep to your ranks and retreat!" Father's voice rang above the din like a trumpet blast. "Hold them! Hold!"

I saw how our men stiffened at the sound of his voice and fought back with new courage.

Then our soldiers forced a gap through the mob of axe men

and two of my father's knights rode ahead. We bolted for safety through that gap. I clung to Elizabeth, my hands wound tightly in her skirts. As we rode, I was desperate to call out to my father, but the only name that came out of my mouth was Elizabeth's.

We dashed down the narrow valley, and the little roan carried us bravely. She made not a single stumble, so intent was she to get as far away from the noise and the smell of blood. Trees rushed by so fast, they blurred like water over a falls. My head hurt, my palms hurt, and I was afraid that I would shame us all by being sick.

We halted with a jolt that made me cry out. The aunts were right behind on borrowed horses and Isabel brought up the rear on her great warhorse. It had a gash in its side but that did not seem to slow it up a bit. When they caught up, we forged ahead.

But blocking our retreat was a band of MacDougall's men who had somehow managed to make their way up the pass to head us off. Two of our knights were stabbing at them with their spears, but they could not reach them all.

Making a run around the longest reaches of our spears, the Highlanders came at us like hungry wolves. Isabel's destrier, a battle-hardened veteran, reared up and lashed out with its hooves, cracking the skull of one man and knocking the axe out of the hands of another.

"To me!" Isabel shouted. "Away to me."

Who was she shouting to? I did not understand. My head had cleared only enough for me to be aware of my fear. My heart pounded against my chest till I thought it would burst, and a cold tremor ran along my arms and legs.

"Give thanks to God!" Elizabeth exclaimed suddenly. "Give thanks to God! It is your father!"

So that was why Isabel was calling out!

I barely had time to take in the sight as my father, his horse thundering up the pass, swept by us and plunged into the fray. Swinging his great axe, and screaming a battle cry, he smashed through the Highlanders like a bull crashing through a paltry hedge. Those who were not slain outright took to their heels in terror.

At last, Father reined in, pausing to catch his breath. Blood dripped from the blade of his short-handled sword. His shield had been so heavily dented by the blows of his enemies, the insignia could no longer be read. I feared if he gave it a good shake, the shield would split in two.

"Father," I whispered.

Only Elizabeth heard me.

Father waved his axe to urge on his spear men who had come running up after him. Turning to one of the knights, a man of some age for his beard was already fully white, he said, "Atholl, get the ladies to safety. Make for Loch Dochart and I'll meet you there. Meanwhile, I'll command the rear guard and keep the MacDougalls back."

Atholl did not look well. Though his axe was bloody from battle, there was a tremor in his left hand and he kept blinking as if the sun was too much for his old eyes. But he acknowledged my father's command with a determined nod and led us away.

So we fled that dreadful valley, more and more homeless vagabonds in our own country.

Father had gambled his great estates for the chance of a crown and now he had lost everything. His kingdom had shrunk to the size of a saddle and the movement of wind across his cheek.

I suddenly remembered how Elizabeth had cautioned that Father and she had been made king and queen after the fashion of children in summer games. But I knew that summer games did not end in blood and the awful screams of horses and men.

"Dear Lord . . ." I began. But I had lost what prayers I had and could only put my head against Elizabeth's back and weep.

18 ❧ THE EIGHTH DAY OF MY CAPTIVITY

The morning is more difficult than the night.

The mob is back, armed with more produce. Now they not only have neeps and tatties, but the bones of sheep, which knock horribly against the bars of my cage. The mob also fling some kind of mud, which lands on the floor of the cage and gives off an awful stink.

I pick some up to throw it back.

Not mud, then, but what a horse or cow has left behind!

What pigs, these English are. God can forgive them if He wants to. I never shall.

Still, after an hour of flinging dung and screaming names, even they tire of the game and leave. I wait till no one is around, then I save what I can of the neeps and tatties. Even raw, they can be filling. I must be careful though. I cannot eat too much of them at one time without a pain in my bowels.

To my delight, there is still some meat on the sheep bones. Surely if I can crack the bones, there will be some marrow inside as well. My enemies did not mean to, but they have left me quite a feast. After eight days of gruel, morning and evening, I feel lucky.

I use the privy bucket to clean my little cage, scrabbling about on my hands and knees. I am like my own servant now.

There is no one else. If I do not care for the cage, I am the only one who will have to live in its filth.

While I clean the cage floor, I think about Longshanks and our strange war of words.

He says he will tell me more tonight.

Perhaps.

Perhaps not.

It is the telling that is important, not the truth of it.

I cling to that thought and smile. "Perhaps, Longshanks, I will tell you some untruths as well. We will see how you like it."

He comes as promised, after the lights in the little cottages are extinguished. Moving like a shadow, he limps over to the cage.

This time he throws back the hood of his cloak so that I may gaze fully upon his face. On his majesty, I suppose. In the light of the half moon his face looks like bone. He is dying, I think. It comforts me.

"Soon, very soon," he hisses, "you will be moved to London."

"London," I repeat slowly. England's capital city, far off to the south. Father has visited there many times, though he has never taken me. London is a long way off, as far away as one can get from Scotland. Can Father follow me there?

For a moment, as Longshanks expects, as he counts on, I consider London.

London could mean a soft bed, decent meals.

London could mean a clean dress, a bath, a friend.

Then I remember who is speaking the words.

Longshanks.

My father's enemy.

And mine.

And I know then that what he says is all lies.

"Yes, London," the snake voice comes again. "For this hamlet is hardly a suitable place to display my greatest prize."

Lanercost a hamlet?

Of course.

It is a waystop. A dimple in the road. A pimple on the backside of the Scottish border.

I think of the grey stone walls of the priory, now made black by night. I think of the small thatched cottages that surround it. Of course Longshanks wants a bigger crowd to view his prize, the Scottish princess. He wants to display me in London alongside mermaids caught off the southern shore, alongside the horns of unicorns, one more rarity for the English to gawk at.

He does not know I have guessed his game. And I will not tell him. I bite my lip.

He waves a hand at the priory and the surrounding countryside. "A few pious monks and some unwashed peasants are a very small audience for such a treasure."

"Treasure," I say.

"London." He smiles. A shadow from the moonlight blacks out his teeth. His mouth is all cavern now. "I am having a fresh cage prepared for you there. It will hang from the Tower of London so that all my court and the whole populace of the city can see you."

"So," I say, "I will still be in a cage!" I make a mock gasp and put my hand to my mouth, but of course I am not surprised.

"Yes. Girl in a cage." His voice is slimy, like a slug's foot. Clearly he believes I had not guessed. "But a nicer cage than this. You will get to see all of London by day, and sleep indoors at night, though your keepers will not be allowed to speak to you."

I can see what he wants.

He wants me to thank him. He wants me to be in his debt. He wants me to grovel and to love him. But I will not.

"I want to stay here," I say. "I like it here. In Lanercost."

The lie nearly chokes me, but I know it is the last thing he expects to hear.

"Stay here?" He cannot keep the shock from his voice. "You will not like it for long. This is October and still mild. But after October comes November and the frost. And sometimes snow. You will not like being in an open cage then."

I turn away and say nothing. If he can use silence against me, I will use it against him. Though I want desperately to know about my aunts, about Father, about the uncles, I say no more. And next time he comes, I will not speak to him at all.

Not a single word.

19 ❧ THE SCOTTISH HIGH-LANDS, AUGUST–SEPTEMBER 1306

We spent that night in a small castle that was on an island in Loch Dochart. I thrilled to see the grey stones of the building, caring little if the inhabitants were friends or foes. Just to be inside by a warm fire with walls to keep out the wind had become my idea of heaven.

Old Atholl said that the bridge that joined the island to the shore was easy to defend and he immediately stationed a man on the battlements to keep watch for trouble.

By the time father joined us, however, he had given the MacDougalls such a bloody nose that they had abandoned the chase. The mood became lighter when this news reached us.

Even my head stopped hurting.

After a meager supper—for the castle had not been prepared for so many mouths to feed—Elizabeth saw to it that the dirt was scrubbed off me. With lavender soap! She combed out my hair with a bone comb and I did not once complain. Then she gently smeared bramble leaves over a bump on my head to bring the swelling down before putting me to bed. All this, and she had taken no time for her own toilette. Her own hair had shaken loose of its careful braiding on our wild ride, and her dress was, if anything, now far dirtier than mine.

I recalled then how she had pressed me to the ground and

shielded me with her own body when the axe man had attacked. So I raised up from my pillow in the little bed I had been given, and kissed both her hands.

For a moment she looked surprised. Then she smiled, her eyes no longer wintry, and kissed me back quickly on the cheek.

Then, without a word, she left. I could hear the sound of her skirts going *swee-swash* along the stone floor.

Father appeared before the sound was entirely gone. He knelt by the bedside and stroked my hair.

"How are you, my brave princess?" he asked.

"I do not feel very brave," I replied.

He laughed, his eyes crinkling at the corners so that it seemed as if old times were at hand. "Oh, feeling has nothing to do with it, Marjorie. It is not like feeling hot or cold, dry or wet. Brave is how you behave."

"Then I did not behave bravely, Father," I admitted. "It was Elizabeth who—"

He stopped me with a finger on my lips. "Elizabeth told me how brave you were," he said.

I yawned. "I just did as I was told."

"Sometimes that is all that courage is," he said. "Just doing what you know you have to do."

Had I been brave then? It was a new idea for me. But I was so tired, I could not think on it any more. The bed was soft, the coverlet warm, and soon my eyes closed without my being able to stop them, and I was sound asleep.

In the morning we were all gathered outside the castle. The horses were watered and fed, and it seemed to me that more care was being taken of them than had been taken of any of us.

I had on a clean dress, which one of the servants had discovered for me. It was a washed-out grey, like the soft wings of a dove. Even though it fit a bit too snugly around the waist than was comfortable, I did not complain. A brave warrior pays no attention to that sort of thing. Besides, neither Elizabeth nor Isabel had fresh clothes, though their dresses had been washed and dried overnight.

Father stood before us in his mail shirt and plain blue cloak, his hair brushed back from his eyes. His skin seemed burnished, as if he had been through a fire, and his mouth was set in a firm line. He looked round at the company and appeared well satisfied with what he saw.

"My friends," he addressed us, his voice filled with warmth, "I call you friends whether you be kinsmen, knights, or soldiers, for I count any man a friend who stands by my side. Things have never looked darker since the day I accepted the crown from the hands of Lady Isabel."

All eyes swung toward Isabel, but her gaze remained fixed upon my father.

"The pain of freedom is better than the comfort of slavery," he went on. "For Scotland is not a crown or a throne or castles or riches. Scotland lives in the hearts of free men who are ready to fight for her, however many or few they may be."

The men broke out into a spontaneous and ragged cheer and Father gave a wry smile in answer.

"We are few enough now, as any of you can see, but *we* are the realm of Scotland and we *will* grow. One day there will be enough of us to strike back at our adversary, Edward Longshanks, who dares call himself 'Hammer of the Scots.' One day—and may it be soon—we will drive his hated armies from our home forever."

A vigorous voice rang out and I was surprised to see it came

from old Atholl. "Long live King Robert!" he cried. "And freedom to Scotland!"

"King Robert and Scotland!" echoed all the men there, so
loudly that for a moment they sounded like a mighty host rather
than a small, beleaguered band.

I shouted along with them and I heard Isabel shout, too.

Father waited for the noise to die down, then took Elizabeth
and me aside, along with his sisters and Isabel.

"I am giving all the horses we have left to Neil and Atholl,"
he said. "They will take you north to Kildrummy Castle by
routes the English will not have reached yet. You will be much
safer there than you are with me. While they look for me, they
will not be looking for you."

"What do you mean to do?" Elizabeth asked. She put a hand
on his arm.

"I will take those men that are still fit and fight my way
through to the west coast. There and among the western isles I
can gather a fresh army and continue the struggle." He spoke to
her, but to all of us as well.

"We could all escape together, you know," Elizabeth said,
her hand tightening on his arm. "To Ireland or Norway. We
could start a new life there away from all this." I could detect no
cowardice in her voice, only concern for him.

My father's said tenderly, "You know I cannot do that, *mon
coeur*. Scotland has a king now and will have as long as I live."

Elizabeth nodded, and took her hand from his arm. "I expected no less of you, my husband, and I shall not fail to be
worthy of your courage. However long we are apart and whatever befalls us, I shall be true to you in every way. I swear it."

He touched a finger to her lips to silence her. "There is no need to swear to that which I already know," he told her. Then he removed his finger and replaced it with a kiss.

He embraced each of us one last time, and whispered to me, "I count on your brave heart, child. You are a Bruce and the best of us."

Then he led everyone across Castle Dochart's bridge to the shore. There we mounted our horses and prepared to turn north. Once more Elizabeth and I were on the little roan mare who had proved so noble in flight.

"Has she a name?" I asked Elizabeth.

She shook her head. "Not that I know."

"May I name her?" She nodded. "Caledonia," I said, speaking the old name for Scotland.

"A fine choice, little Jo," she answered.

Uncle Neil raised his arm in salute to Father and the men who were by his side, then wheeled about. We followed with our escort, no more than a dozen horsemen.

The last sight I had of my father was his lifted arm, waving farewell to us from the midst of his brave band.

20 ¸ THE SCOTTISH HIGHLANDS, AUGUST– SEPTEMBER 1306

On this part of the journey, I promised myself to look only at the sky, not at the sheer drops of the cliffs on our left. Above us eagles soared, wheeling on their endless rounds in the sky. It was more difficult to keep that promise when we descended into the deep glens. Those glens were constantly in shadow, with icy water trickling into them from the snowy peaks above. Birch and rowan and oak interlaced above us, making night of day. The glens were mysterious and terrifying. I wondered what dark secrets they held. But the cliffs were more frightening still. If I had not been so scared by the heights, I might have marveled at the beauty around me. But all I could think of was the danger.

Thank goodness for the surefootedness of our horses! There was rarely a misstep as we went along.

For a while I rode with Isabel, but she seemed to like the heights and kept insisting I look down.

"It is like anything dangerous. If you do it enough, little Jo," she said with a laugh, "you will soon find that you prefer it."

I shook my head.

"Do it!" she commanded. "Be like those eagles overhead. Ride the changing winds."

I tried. But in looking down, all I succeeded in doing was to make myself so sick, I had to get off her horse and lean against the cliff while I threw up what little was in my stomach.

How is this brave? I thought. I worried that I was not Bruce enough for my father and that I had shamed myself before the one woman I had hoped to please.

Isabel rode on ahead with the men and did not look back.

Elizabeth insisted that I ride with her again and I found I did not mind it as I once did. After all, hadn't Father said that bravery sometimes consisted of doing what I was told?

We found a small meadow in one of the glens. It was one of the few places where sunlight had found a purchase and we were happy in its warmth. Uncle Neil had us get down off the horses and stretch a bit. I lifted my skirts and ran around the periphery of the green like a colt let out to pasture.

When I got back to the others, Isabel was saying testily to Uncle Neil, "We should be going faster, not resting here like a warren of rabbits ready to be collected by a poacher."

Uncle Neil smiled, but there was a deep wariness in his eyes. "We go carefully," he said. "Lest we fall into bad company, Isabel."

"What *company*?" Isabel challenged, her hands firmly on her hips. "Look around, Neil. We are desperately alone here."

"And we must stay that way till we reach Kildrummy," he replied. "We cannot tell friend from foe here in the Highlands, so it is best we rely only on ourselves. You are too reckless, woman. Even rabbits are wary in the field."

It was to be the first of a series of quarrels among us.

As day turned to night and then day again, we all began getting on one another's nerves. What had seemed comfortable, familiar, reliable, suddenly became dangerously tiresome— even annoying. Aunt Mary's sweetness began to grate. Aunt Christina's fussiness drew sharp responses. Uncle Neil's leadership was challenged often by Atholl. Atholl lectured and postured and spoke of how things used to be. Then Elizabeth and Isabel began to quarrel, sharply and often.

And everyone—*everyone*—complained about me.

I was too slow, I was too quick; I was too noisy, I was too quiet; I was in the way, I was not around to help; I was eating too much, I was not eating enough. And it seemed as if Isabel found the most wrong with me. If I had loved her before, I think I hated her then.

Around the fourth evening, when we had stopped and made camp, I walked away from the others and gazed up at the sky. I saw a single eagle flying between the distant peaks. His sharp cry sounded brave and lonely all at once and it made me think of Father making his way through hostile territory.

"Oh, Father," I whispered, staring up at the bird, "I wish you could fly to safety as we seem to be doing, so high above the tree line." I missed Father dreadfully. Not the way I used to miss him when he was off in England checking on his lands. That had been a childish, selfish kind of missing. This was different. This was a fear rooted deep in the bone, like a sickness that would not heal. A fear that I would never see him again.

Of course I was certain Uncle Neil could keep *us* safe. But it was not my own safety I worried about.

It was Father's.

I looked away from the eagle and turned back to join the others at the campfire.

Elizabeth stared at me as if she could guess what I was thinking. There was a question on her face, but she did not ask it.

And I—I did not speak of my fears, as if naming them would call them onto Father's head. But my silence was echoed by the silence around me.

Clearly everyone had the same worry.

Now we were moving too quickly to do much hunting along the way. Most days—after a long, hard, cold ride—all we had to look forward to when we made camp was a bitter soup made from boiled nettles. I hated the stuff and could barely get it down. Only the fact that my stomach clenched with hunger allowed me to drink it.

All of us grew thinner day by day. The grey dress, once so tight on me, now hung in folds.

All of us were covered with ticks and fleas. We scratched at ourselves like dogs.

Aunts Mary and Christina had lost enough weight, Uncle Neil said, to have made another sister between them. I laughed at that till I cried, and then laughed again.

Isabel had come out in freckles from so much wind and sun. Uncle Neil had fined down to knobs and muscle.

In Elizabeth's case, the fear and hunger had burned all the dullness out of her. For the first time I could see the strength that my father must have loved from the beginning. She had the bones and beauty of a saint.

But Old John of Atholl fared the worst of us all. He had developed a dry cough for which the only sure remedy seemed to be a shot of whiskey each morning and night, though Aunt Christina had offered to make a tonic of alder bark, which he declined. Elizabeth rationed the whiskey out, saving all for him.

Nonetheless, Atholl insisted on riding at the front of our little band alongside Uncle Neil, the first to face any danger that might lie in wait.

"As the king would have me do," he said, coughing three times in that short declaration.

Whenever we stopped to make camp, Elizabeth was quick to take charge. She assigned tasks to everyone: gathering firewood, tending the horses, making the fire.

"Marjorie," she would say to me, "get water from the spring," or "set out the pots." I was always quick to obey. In that much, at least, I suppose I was brave.

Above all, Elizabeth always made sure that Atholl was well tended, with blankets and a drink heated over the campfire.

The old man tried to protest, but Elizabeth said the one thing certain to shut him up.

"As the king would have *me* do," she told him in a tone that gave him no room for argument.

The journey seemed endless, and just when I thought I could bear no more, we emerged from a great forest onto open ground. Uncle Neil reined us in and pointed. "There. Kildrummy."

And there indeed, a mile or so ahead of us—was a castle.

It was built upon a ridge and looked down on the land below from an impressive height. It was much grander than Lochmaben, grander even than Stirling. There was a fortified gatehouse, two forward towers with lookouts on top, and two huge towers at the back. A long grey slope of roof covered the great hall.

I clapped my hands. The place looked so inviting. And so safe. "Kildrummy," I whispered, liking the sound of it.

With Uncle Neil and Atholl in the lead, we wound down the hill. The horses' heads were up for the first time in days, as if they smelled fresh hay, and as I sat behind Elizabeth on little Caledonia, she practically danced beneath us.

All of a sudden I grew wary. "Are we sure this castle is held by friends?"

"It belongs to the earls of Mar," Elizabeth explained. "Your own mother was born here."

"Oh." For a moment I felt stupid. There seemed so much history in Scotland and I knew so little of it. I renewed my promise to myself to study that I might be worthy of the title of princess.

We approached Kildrummy across a causeway that spanned a broad ditch. The walls reared high above our heads and I could see that the towers were dotted with arrow slits. Those slits would allow the castle's defenders to rain missiles down upon anybody who dared attack.

Woe betide Edward Longshanks, I thought, *if he tries to attack us here.*

The iron gate was raised with a rattle of chains and we proceeded into a wide courtyard where a small group of men, armored and armed, were waiting to greet us.

"Praise God you have arrived, Neil!" exclaimed their leader, a tall man with white-gold hair beneath a silver helmet. His face was sharp, and there was the look of a hungry wolf about him. Fixing his gaze on Uncle Neil, he asked urgently, "What news of the king?"

"He fights on for Scotland, wherever he may be, Durward," Uncle Neil replied. "And that is all that is safe for anyone to know. What you do not know will not be gotten from you."

Durward nodded.

"But what news have you of the English?" Uncle Neil asked.

Durward shook his head. "Pembroke has reached Aberdeen."

Elizabeth gasped and her hand went up to her throat. "So far north?"

Nodding, Durward added, "And much too close to here for comfort, ma'am." He turned back to Uncle Neil. "When last heard of, Pembroke was waiting there for the Prince of Wales to join him with his siege engines so that they can shatter the castle—"

At this Isabel interrupted. "Wales is a prickasour," she said and flipped her long braid off her shoulder. "He has little belly for war. Not like his father. He will not know what to do when he encounters real Scots. Probably run and hide behind Papa Longshanks' shield." She laughed and jumped down from her horse without help.

I had little belly for war, too. But I had never heard that said of the English before.

"He may not know what to do, my lady," Durward said pleasantly enough, though his wolf-face was never less than wary. "But his generals know all too well. Do not discount the prince yet. He may even listen to his generals and that will not help us at all."

"Are you apologizing for the English?" Isabel said.

There was a shocked silence.

Even I knew better than to put a stick in the eye of a wolf.

Elizabeth kicked our little horse forward, effectively blocking Isabel from the rest of the Kildrummy company. "We are grateful to the Earl of Mar for this refuge, my lord."

Durward turned to officially greet her, saying, "I am Sir Alan. And this home is yours for as long as you need it, Majesty." He helped her down from the horse, then turned and helped Aunts Mary and Christina. I jumped down the way Isabel had.

Immediately grooms took charge of our weary horses. They tried not to notice how filthy we were, but it was in their eyes.

A maid, not much older than I was, bowed low before Elizabeth and said, "Your Majesty, you are all to be quartered in the Snow Tower, in the chambers used by the earl's family."

"The Snow Tower?" I asked warily. "Is it so cold?"

"Not at all. It is quite the best the castle has to offer." Without another word, she led the way toward the tower entrance.

"This is the tower?" I gasped. It was seven stories high, with a gallery that connected it to the Great Hall.

The maid seemed to be galloping along and all I wanted to do was stand and stare at the place. But the others would have soon left me behind and I had to hurry to catch up.

Once inside the tower, we wound our way up a spiral stairway, the stones of the risers much worn with age.

"Why is it called the *Snow*—?" I began again.

She smiled and interrupted me. "This will be your chamber, Princess." She halted at one door and pushed it wide open.

I stepped inside.

The room smelled of sandalwood and beeswax candles; it smelled of fresh rushes and rose petals on the floor.

On the walls were great hangings, all winter scenes: huntsmen trailing through an icy forest carrying a dead wolf, a robin perched upon a white hedge, deer floundering in steep drifts.

There was a picture of Our Lord's nativity, the roof of the stable encrusted with frost and angels descending from the stars on swanlike wings.

In the midst of this snowy room two braziers burned, their blazing coals casting a cheery glow across a carpet decorated with snowdrops and white lilies. I had stepped into a fairy world where both summer and winter reigned side by side.

A metal bathtub sat in the center of the room between the two braziers.

"The water for your bath will be here presently," the maid said. "Now I will show the other ladies to their rooms."

I sighed out loud and they all laughed, but I did not care. *A bath!* I did not care how cold the pictures were on the hangings, I would make it summer in my room.

It was not long before a train of servants arrived carrying great kettles of water that were heated over an open fire in the kitchen and had to be brought up to the tower in relays. They filled the tub and, as soon as I was alone, I stripped off my filthy clothes and slipped in. Lying back, I watched the steam rise up to the ceiling, where wooden panels were painted with doves in flight.

I thought again of the eagle soaring over the mountain. Then I remembered the steep drops and what they did to my stomach.

I decided I preferred the doves.

I fell asleep in the tub and woke up shivering in the cold water. I got out and wrapped myself in a soft robe and then saw what had been laid out on the bed. My horrible grey dress was gone but in its place was a soft green woolen under-dress, fitted closely at the bust and with long loose sleeves and a gold-colored belt. And because it was cold up here in Kildrummy, despite it being September, there was a cotte of green brocade to go over it.

I put it all on and spun about on my tiptoes. For the first time since the coronation I felt like a princess.

And I was clean.

Clean!

I made my way down the tower stairs and across to the main part of the castle and wandered about till I found the rest of my company. They were all gathered in the Great Hall.

It was an enormous room with a vaulted ceiling some three stories tall. At one end, near the fireplace, a table had been laid out with good plain food.

I sat between Elizabeth and Uncle Neil in a seat they had been saving for me.

"Slugabed," Uncle Neil teased.

"I was taking a bath," I said. I held up a strand of my hair, still slightly damp.

"You look lovely," Elizabeth commented.

No sooner had I sat down then my trencher was piled high with a slab of venison, plus a large serving of boar surrounded by pears and chestnuts. Uncle Neil tore off a hunk of good brown bread and handed it to me. I dipped it in the meat juices and did not even mind when some of it ran down my chin.

Every mouthful tasted both sweet and salt together. *Heaven!* I thought.

Afterward, the servants brought in cheeses for digestion and hot spiced wine. But I had eaten so little for so long, I had to stop before cleaning my platter. My poor shrunken belly was aching and had already stretched beyond its capacity.

Sir Alan raised his goblet high. "To the royal family," he said. "May God protect you all, and good King Robert, wherever he may be."

"To the king!" we all shouted.

I turned to grin at Elizabeth. Her face closed in on itself. I wondered why. Here we were, safe at last in the stony arms of Kildrummy. We were way out of Edward Longshanks' reach.

And then I understood. Elizabeth was concerned for Father. We were safe—but he was not. We were freshly bathed with full plates before us, soon to sleep in soft beds. Father was camped among the hills and trees, dodging his enemies at every turn.

I reached over and touched her hand. It was cool under my fingers. I whispered, "It is not fair, I know. But Father would wish us these small comforts now."

She turned and stared at me for a moment. "You have grown, child," she said. Then she picked up her knife and began to eat.

21 ❧ THE NINTH DAY OF MY CAPTIVITY

The morning hours seemed to crawl along, like a legless beggar in a town square. I swear, I would even welcome a mob of howling English if only to relieve my boredom.

I pace my cage, like a beast too long in captivity. My legs are weak from inactivity. My fingers ache to be doing something, even embroidery, which is not among my favorite things. My mouth is barren of words. Lord, I am hungry for company, for companionship.

The monk who brought my morning meal did not speak to me, of course. Nor did any of the guards. I long for evening when Longshanks will come. At least in not talking to him, I will have something to occupy my time.

Surprisingly, at the noon bell, Longshanks comes out of the priory.

Thank you, Lord, that my wait has been shortened.

Then I warn myself, over and over—like a soldier training for battle—"Say not a word to him. Say not a word."

He is carried in an open litter by four strong men. His peacock of a servant walks by his side, in a bright yellow brocade surcoat with embroidery on the sleeves.

Behind the litter come two clever-looking men in dark robes. I suppose they are his physicians. They confer with one another in hushed whispers. Every few moments one of them tilts his head in the direction of the royal patient.

Do they know how sick he is? How can they not know? He is yellow with his illness.

A group of soldiers follows behind the physicians. Like Noah's animals, they march in pairs. I count twelve of them. They are armed with pikes and do not speak a word. They seem ready for some sort of attack.

Well, I am ready, too. Ready for my own battle with Longshanks.

"Come closer," I whisper, "so I may show you the shield of my silence."

But as if he guesses my intent, his litter does not come near my cage.

In the strong light of day, the yellow cast to his skin is now grey. The hair that peeks out from under his cap is the color of weathered stone. He hunches over as if instead of a crown he wears a stone.

I try to catch his eye but he looks away. One hand has dropped over the side of the litter and moves back and forth like the tail of a fish.

For a moment I wonder if Longshanks is ashamed of what he has done to me. But I do not think so. He is not a man who would ever own up to shame. Perhaps kings dare not do so as it would make them seem weak.

Suddenly I remember Father on his knees before the abbot, shamed because he had killed an enemy in a holy place. Maybe it takes a stronger king than Longshanks to admit that he has been wrong.

So, then, it is not all kings who act like Longshanks. It is an interesting thought.

Suddenly I feel pity for that sick old man. He feels he must bear his infirmities without complaint in front of his strong young soldiers. He pursues a war while ill unto death, without chance to rest or recover or even die peacefully in his own bed. He raises the dragon and cages girls and fights women—all shameful things. And he feels he must not admit the shame of it.

Really, I think, Longshanks is as much caged as I.

And then I shake my head. He has chosen his cage. His battles. His war.

And mine.

For a while I am upset at the missed moment. I did not have the chance to shame Longshanks even more with my silence. But then I realize, there is still evening to come.

And Longshanks will be there. It is part of his war. He will not deny himself the pleasure of taunting Robert the Bruce's child.

The monk comes at last with my supper and I realize, suddenly, that I am truly starving. I wonder if planning a war always makes one hungry.

As usual he passes me my meager meal without a word, then starts to leave.

I will be using silence with Longshanks, but I have no quarrel with this man of God. I decide to speak to him.

Before he has gone more than a pace, I put a hand through the bars and say in my sweetest voice, "Pray, stay a while yet, kind brother." It is the very tone I use to use to wheedle treats out of my father. "The night is coming on and I am a child afraid of the dark. My mother and father are far from here so I have no other comfort, brother, but you."

He does not look back but his steps slow.

I lean against the bars as if I could melt through them. "Are you forbidden to give me your company? You could do that and still keep silence." I make my voice small, barely audible.

He moves on again. In his life he must have denied himself many things and the habit of obedience runs deep in his soul. I need something more to sway him.

But what?

Conscience!

That is it! I must reach the monk's conscience.

I try to recall what Father Alberic back in Lochmaben tried to teach me. I was usually so bored with him and his droning voice, I stared out the window rather than paying attention. Or I teased the cat with a bit of embroidery thread.

Suddenly, as though an angel just opened a door in my memory, it comes to me.

Charity.

I raise my voice.

"Is not one of the acts of charity to visit prisoners?"

This time he halts in midstep.

"Acts of charity," I continue, recalling the lesson now. "There are seven." I count on my fingers. Along the ground, my shadow counts shadow fingers, too. "Firstly, tending the sick, then feeding the hungry. Next, giving drink to the thirsty, clothes to the naked, harboring strangers." I shift hands. "Burying the dead." I draw a deep breath, lean away from the bars, then say the seventh, "And bringing comfort to prisoners." I smile, having remembered them all.

The monk has remained poised on the same spot, his fingers rubbing the prayer beads that hang from the cord at his waist.

"Can someone order you to break God's commandments?" I ask. "Can even King Edward . . ."—it hurts me to give Longshanks his title, but I do—"can King Edward order you to go against God's will?"

And then, like a huge galleon swinging slowly about in the harbor before making its way out to sea, the monk turns back toward me.

I feel the impulse to spur him on, to keep gabbling at him. Yet I put a hand to my mouth to stop my tongue. One wrong word now could undo all that I have accomplished.

When he reaches the cage, sailing across the yard, he perches himself on the edge of the platform. His head is down as if he is contemplating the earth. I notice the hair around his tonsure, which is thin and slightly grey. He may look as if he is watching the earth, but I guess he is thinking about Heaven.

I move close to him, so close that we would be snuggled together, were it not for the bars of the cage. Taking a spoonful of the gruel he had just left me, I smile as though I am enjoying the food.

He stares at his lap and toys nervously with his prayer beads.

Suddenly I cannot think what to say. I take a sip of water and clear my throat.

"Lanercost priory looks so grand," I say at last, as if we were sitting at the table in a king's castle and making polite conversation. "Is it very old?"

He touches a finger to his lips and shakes his head.

I put my own finger to my lips. "You are not allowed to speak to me?"

He nods.

"That is all right, brother," I say softly. "All I want is a little company. I do not mind doing all the talking."

He nods again, his pleasant face held tight. There is a tic in the corner of his left eye.

So I lean slightly away from him and speak of ordinary things: of growing up in Lochmaben, of Maggie teaching me to sing, of my lessons with Father Alberic, of my little rug made in Flanders. I tell him how in Scotland we eat our porridge with salt, not honey. I tell him of my hawk, whose name is Ranger, whom I have had since I was big enough to carry her on my arm. I tell him how Uncle Neil taught me to dance.

I do not speak of my father or Longshanks or the war going on between them. I do not mention history or the monarchy at all.

All the while he watches me out of the corner of his eye. And, slowly, as I keep on speaking, the tic goes away.

I expect he is waiting till my meal is done, so I talk more than I eat, trying to make the gruel last longer. Because the longer he sits with me, the more I have made him mine.

"I suppose I am not really alone," I say, scraping the last of my supper from the bowl. "Not as long as God is with me. But He is a very quiet companion, brother. Just like you."

The monk still speaks not a word. He collects my dish and spoon and makes his shuffling way back to the priory, his robes rustling slightly.

But we both know that he listened to me. He has found that I am a child, not a monster. That I am small and godly and alone.

Now as night falls, I am no longer in despair. If I can win this small victory here in my cage, perhaps I can win others.

"It is a slender thread of hope," I whisper to myself. "So slender even a spider could not swing from it."

But it is all I have.

For now, it is enough.

22 ❧ THE TENTH DAY OF MY CAPTIVITY

For the first time since being put in the cage, I sleep well. I do not even wait up for Longshanks, but fall asleep soon after the monk leaves. My dreams are simple reminders of home.

I wake in the brisk October morning with a song of Maggie's running through my mind. When I push aside the privy curtain, I see that the sun is weak and the bars of my cage are like shadows.

I put a hand to them. They may look like shadows, but, thin as they are, they are as firm as ever.

My wrists sticking out of the sleeves of my filthy dress are the same: thin and firm.

When the monk comes with my meal—that unappetizing gruel—he looks directly at me for the first time.

"Good morning, brother," I say.

There is a softening of his features. Where yesterday he had a slash of line for lips, now the line is rounder, suggesting pity. His blue eyes are no longer distant skies, but the closer blue of water. He smoothes a hand down his brown robe, but—of course—does not speak.

I smile at him and am comforted by my own smile.

He stays for a moment longer than necessary, and I tell him how I learned to play draughts from the cook.

"It was not long," I say, "till I was winning every other game. Cook said I had a natural talent."

He does not move away.

"My favorite color is green," I say, touching the skirt that was once so brilliantly green.

He smiles at that, and I guess it is his favorite, too.

So I add softly, "It is kind of you to sit with me." I pause and shake my head. "But I am lonely so much of the time when you are not here. I do wish I had a book to keep me company. I could imagine someone's voice saying the words as I read, as though they were there talking to me. Any sort of book would do. Stories, poems, songs. A prayer book."

He does not answer, but his face softens even more, as if in thought.

Or in prayer.

The morning flies by as I go over and over my conversation with the monk.

I wonder: Can it be called a conversation when only one person speaks?

And then I tell myself that he may not have said a word, but his body spoke volumes. The tic at his eye, the softening of his mouth, the eyes whose color seemed to change—that was conversation, too.

If I am to be silent in Longshanks' presence, my body must be mute as well.

Which will be harder, I wonder—the mouth's silence, or the body's? I expect I will find out soon enough, for Longshanks has returned from his morning outing.

He orders his men to halt in a voice that trembles. As he

clambers out of the litter by himself, I can see the pain lines that spread across his face. They are like cracks in broken glass.

I sit down on the floor of the cage, cross-legged, my hands clasped as if in prayer. In fact I keep them that way so they will not shake.

He walks toward me slowly and deliberately. His legs are so long, he looks like a human grasshopper. When he reaches the cage he takes a deep breath before speaking.

"You do not look well," he comments wryly.

I do not answer him. Filthy as I am, thin as I am, I know I look better than he does. I stare at the far wall of bars. And through them.

There is a noise beside me, an odd scraping. Through the corners of my eyes I see that Longshanks is gripping the bars. We both know he does it because otherwise he might fall down. But I say nothing.

"I have had a good outing," he says. "I grow stronger while you grow weaker, girl."

We both know this is a lie but I do not respond. My hands are clasped together so hard, the fingers have gone numb.

He sags against the bars. "Soon I will be in the saddle, finishing off the last of this minor rebellion, this miserable uprising, this paltry rumble."

So many words for something he professes to despise. My hands are cold but they no longer want to tremble.

"Pah, girl, your small attempt at fighting me with silence is as futile as your father's small war. Look where you are and where I am."

Clearly my silence annoys him. I bite my lower lip. I will not think about my father, or his small war.

"I have had dogs better trained than you."

My bottom hurts. My knees ache. There is a slight itch at the end of my nose. Still I do not move.

"I had a hound once," he says, "who was great in the field." His voice is steady but his knuckles around the bars are white. "But once he did not bring to me the rabbit I shot, and I beat him. The next time he tried such a thing, I had him hanged." He smiles slowly, knowing that I know he is talking about men, not dogs, that he is talking about my father. He is talking about me.

I am careful not to respond.

"Do not think your little game of silence will win you anything. This is once, girl." He held up one finger. "There will be no second chance. As I am with dogs, I am with little girls."

The silence stretches between us. It is as real as a wall.

Finally, tired of this, he says, "I have no patience with your nonsense. The business of kingship is too serious for that."

I smile inwardly. But not on my mouth. Longshanks is lying, of course. He has plenty of time for this nonsense. Otherwise, why does he come again and again to speak to me?

"You think perhaps your father will rescue you? You think that he is free?" Longshanks scoffed.

I go cold. Has he come then to tell me Father has been captured? Without meaning to, I lean toward him.

"He is no more free than you are. The sea bounds him on three sides while I hold the fourth. Scotland is not his kingdom but his cage."

Not captured then. I lean back, away from him. Whatever else he has to tell me, it is not what I most fear. I can bear anything if Father is still free.

"Speak, damn you," he says.

I think about what I will say if I choose to speak. I think

about it for a long time. I choose my words carefully. I go over them again and again in my head.

Just as Longshanks is gathering himself to stand, I finally open my mouth.

"If Father's kingdom is a cage, then my cage will be a kingdom," I declare. "It is not I who am locked in, but you who are locked out."

Edward smirks. He has made me speak. He thinks he has won. "What nonsense. You are a vexatious child."

By that I know that my words have wounded him.

And I see now that it is not silence that will win this war between us. That is only a skirmish, a game, like playing draughts with the cook. But I spoke a greater truth to Longshanks when I said that this cage is my kingdom. And I am the royal princess of Lanercost Cage.

If I can truly make it so, I will beat him forever.

The sun is now high overhead. It has been hours since the old man left, all but carried to his litter. I have paced the cage for hours, thinking about what went on between us.

A little brown bird, tidy and neat, flies into the cage and hops around, looking for any food I might have dropped.

Food! As if porridge, water, raw tatties, and neeps can be considered food.

For a moment I remember the last good food I had, the feast at Kildrummy, sitting between Elizabeth and Uncle Neil. I can almost smell the venison and boar that I was too full to finish.

I shake my head, furious with myself. Nothing comes of such remembering except pain. I must look forward, not back, or I will bring tears to my eyes. And Longshanks will consider each tear a victory.

So, once again I consider: If I am to be the royal princess of the Kingdom of Lanercost Cage, what do I need most? Not thrones or ministers or scrolls of the law. Not great feasts or dances or lovely clothes.

I run a hand down the filthy skirt that was once such a lovely green and sigh.

No, what I need in my cage kingdom is a court first. Folk to serve me as I am servant to their needs.

And I will need a chaplain who will listen to my confession.

I know who will be my chaplain. Have I not already confessed my love of the color green to him, among other secrets? Of course he is bound to silence because of that. The silence of the confessional. But he is mine because of it.

It is my courtiers who are the problem. Who can they be and why are they silent?

And then I have it—they can not speak to me without my permission, of course. My royal permission.

All this thinking, all this planning has been exhausting. I curl into a ball on the floor of the cage and try to nap.

Something tugging at my collar wakes me with a start. Fearing another rat, I reach down and take off my shoe. But I do not sit up, do not open my eyes yet. I am stealth complete, and . . .

"Shhh!" says a voice. "I think the guard be napping, but I canna be sure."

I sit up and see it is the girl who talked to me before. The hungry one.

"You," I say stupidly, dropping my shoe.

"Enid," she whispers and puts a finger to her mouth. "I'm called Enid. I've brought ye a bite to eat because ye said ye be hungry."

"But that was days ago."

"I didna believe ye. But I been watchin'," she tells me. "They feed ye less than me."

Gingerly—as if I am a wild beast in this cage—she hands me a tiny bundle wrapped in cloth. I unfold it carefully. It contains a crust of bread and a small piece of cheese. The smell is wonderful, better than any dinner in a Great Hall. I tell her so.

"I saved it from my supper," she said. "I'll be needing the clout back or my ma'll miss it."

I hand over the cloth through the bars. "Thank you," I say. "I did not mean to take your own food away. You said you were hungry, too."

The girl shrugs. "God tells us we mun help the unfortunates," she says. "And I never seen no one so unfortunate in my life before, girl in a cage. Go on. Eat."

I try to take a small bite of the cheese, but it is so dry it starts to crumble in my hand. I have to put it in my mouth all at once so as not to lose any. But one tiny piece falls to the cage floor. I pick it up and stuff it into my already crowded mouth.

The cheese, sharp with age, is wonderful.

Enid seems to enjoy watching me, so I take my time with the bread. That isn't difficult as it needs a lot of chewing.

As I chew, she whispers, "When harvest's bad and we be too hungry to sleep, Ma sometimes tells us tales. 'One day,' she says, 'ye'll all be princes and princesses. And it'll be a better world and all will have plenty o' food and fine clothes.' I never believed that till I saw ye. Yer as skinny and dirty as me and yer a princess, so may happen one day I'll be one, too."

"Maybe you will be," I agree. That brings a smile to her face. Her teeth are the color of old moss. "For now, though, you can be one of my ladies-in-waiting."

"What's 'at?"

"It means you travel around with the princess and live in her house, and help her dress—"

"Oh, yes!" Enid bursts out before I can finish. "Ye'll be princess and I'll be one of your ladies." She puts a finger to her mouth as if afraid she has said too much.

I put my face against the bars. "And a very pretty one, too," I tell her. My face burns with the lie. She is dirty and ratty.

Now she looks abashed, then hopeful, then blushes. "Do ye think so?"

I stare at her little oval of a face, covered with dirt and grime. I see the moss-colored teeth and the greasy hair. I take in the bony arms and the callused hands. I realize her whole life has been one of hard work and drudgery.

I take a deep breath.

"Yes, I do," I say, and mean it. "You are both pretty and strong. From now on you will be Lady Enid."

"Lady Enid," she repeats, rolling the words around on her tongue like a pair of juicy berries. She giggles and curtsies.

"Shhh!" I warn, this time fingers to my own lips.

She nods and looks around.

"You had best get back, Lady Enid, before anyone notices you are gone."

She scurries off, waving to me as she runs.

We are lucky no one else is about, for Enid could be scolded, beaten—even executed—for being my pretend lady. For being one of Longshanks' dogs who does not obey him.

I must be careful.

For Enid's sake, if not my own.

23 ❧ KILDRUMMY CASTLE, THE SCOTTISH HIGH-LANDS, SEPTEMBER 1306

I was allowed to sleep late into the morning in the Snow Tower. By the time I was up and dressed—once again in the soft green wool—everyone else had breakfasted.

As soon as I had eaten—two duck eggs and hot porridge—I ran off to find Uncle Neil. Various servants directed me to different parts of the castle, and so I had what amounted to a tour of all the floors. I found him at last out on the battlements of the southeast tower talking with Elizabeth. There was a soft wind in the trees, and overhead a buzzard was harassing a golden eagle.

"They have arrived much sooner than we anticipated," Uncle Neil was saying as I got close. "They must have marched by night to get here so quickly."

Their attention was fixed on something to the east, so I went over to the wall and stood on tiptoe to peer over. At once I saw what was troubling them—a small knot of horsemen had gathered on one of the far-off hills.

"Marjorie, what are you doing here?" Elizabeth asked sharply.

I stepped back but before I did so, I noticed that a line of spear men had appeared behind the riders.

"Is it Father?" I asked.

"No." Elizabeth shook her head. "It is the English."

I blinked. The English. They looked very small and unthreatening from so far away, and I turned to say so. Before I could get a word out, Uncle Neil leaned even farther over the parapet.

I turned back and saw that what had been one line of spear men had, in a moment, become twenty. As I watched, more and more of them came over the hilltops and began streaming down the slopes below.

"Oh," I whispered, suddenly understanding. These were not the axe men from the Highlands, wild and undisciplined. These were Longshanks' men. First there had seemed only dozens of them, then suddenly hundreds!

"I see the banner of the Prince of Wales," Uncle Neil said. His voice had a funny catch in it. He ran a hand through his hair. "He must have taken personal command."

I could not bear to watch the soldiers and looked up instead. Overhead the buzzard had sent off the eagle and was now in sole command of the sky.

"Isn't it said that Wales is not much of a soldier?" Elizabeth sounded a note of hope.

"He has an army of knights, footmen, and archers, greater than anything we can send against him. And generals—if he will listen to them."

I looked at the two of them and tried to say something brave. "This castle seems very strong. Surely it will stand." But my voice sounded thin.

Uncle Neil rubbed his chin as he eyed the enemy forces. His signet ring winked at me in the sun.

"*Can* the castle stand?" Elizabeth asked.

"It is as strong a fortress as ever I have seen," said Uncle Neil.

It was no answer and Elizabeth asked him again. "But will it *stand?*"

"The English will be hard pressed to take it," he said. "But we have little chance of reinforcements or relief."

"Then we must trust in God," said Elizabeth.

Uncle Neil drew in a deep breath. "In God and in Robert's wisdom."

Elizabeth bit on her lower lip as though she were chewing on a hard decision. "You mean us to flee Scotland then?"

Leave Scotland? My jaw dropped. *But where would we go?*

Uncle Neil put his hand on hers. "You know Robert's first concern—and mine—is for your safety and for Marjorie's. We must get you away from Kildrummy as fast as possible. Longshanks' army must not capture you here." He gestured with his head toward the English far below.

So, I thought, *he does not expect Kildrummy to stand.* I began to tremble.

"You had this planned already," Elizabeth scolded.

Uncle Neil looked down for a moment, then up again. "Durward and I spoke of it, yes. We knew it might come to this. But not . . . not so soon."

She shook her head at him. "I do not like it."

He gestured with his right hand to the armies assembling below. "Think, Elizabeth, think! What would Robert do if you were taken?"

Elizabeth nodded slowly, her hands clasped before her. "You are right. I am being foolishly stubborn. I shall take Marjorie, Mary, and Christina and head north to Orkney." She put a hand to my arm and my trembling ceased.

"Orkney?" I asked. "Where is that?"

"It is an island in the far north," said Elizabeth. "Part of the kingdom of Norway."

"We Bruces are related by marriage to King Haakon of Norway," Uncle Neil explained. He picked me up and held me close, and spoke into my hair. "He will give you protection for as long as is necessary."

All at once I remembered the story he had told me about Margaret, the Maid of Norway, and how she had died on her way to Scotland. I had a sudden and unreasoned fear that if I were to go there I, too, would die before I ever returned.

"No," I said back to him, "I want to stay here, Uncle Neil. I *have* to stay here."

"You heard Neil. It is not safe for us to remain." Elizabeth was stern, unyielding.

"But we just *got* here." I could not keep misery from my voice.

Uncle Neil set me down again and Elizabeth bent slightly to look me directly in the eye. She spoke simply, as if to an infant. "It is for your father's sake that we must go. If we are captured, then Edward can use us as a weapon. We would be hostages to Robert's good behavior. He would give up *all* for us. You understand that, don't you?"

I nodded numbly. By *all*, she meant his very life.

"Good. We must both try to be as brave as your father."

"Braver," Uncle Neil said and gave me a grin, but I was not fooled for a minute.

"Are you not coming with us, Uncle Neil?" I asked.

"Someone has to hold the castle, little Jo," he said, smiling, though it never quite reached his eyes. "And make them think you are still within. I will catch up as soon as we have beaten them."

Elizabeth gathered us all together and Aunts Mary and Christina looked as downcast as I felt. Only Isabel showed any relish for this fresh journey.

"We have led those knaves a merry chase," Isabel said, tucking her red braid behind her. She clapped her hands. "This time we will outstrip them for good." Grinning, she squeezed my shoulder, and I felt a share of her courage flowing into me.

"Enough talk," Elizabeth told us. "We must hurry." She chivvied us down the back stairs like a dog with sheep.

We ran before her, lifting our skirts so as not to trip on the steps.

Our horses, newly shod by a weasel-faced blacksmith named Osbourne, had already been taken to a small back gate and led down the slope to wait for us, part of Uncle Neil's escape plan. The kitchen staff had packed small saddle bags with food and water for the journey, and Elizabeth had us check them all.

Isabel ran back up the stairs.

"Now where is she off to?" Elizabeth asked. She could not keep the annoyance from her voice.

Minutes later Isabel returned, carrying a short sword. "I could not go without this," she explained.

"I wish I had one, too," I told her.

"When we are far from here, I shall teach you how to hold mine," she said. "It is heavier than you can imagine."

Just then Uncle Neil came down to us. He was fully dressed

for war in mail shirt, gauntlets, and helmet. He kissed his sisters and then picked me up and swung me around, clanking as he moved. He seemed relieved that we were going—and so quickly.

When he put me down, he turned to Elizabeth. "Now here is the rest of the plan. I will lead a sally against the enemy before they can form up properly and encircle the castle. That way, we can force them to withdraw and give you more time for your escape."

Elizabeth nodded.

Isabel added, "A good plan. I like it."

"And then will you follow us?" I asked.

"No, sweetling," he said, "I must hold the castle for as long as I am able, so the villains will think you and the queen are still here."

Elizabeth put her hand in his. "We will take John of Atholl to guide us and no more than that," she told him. "He has already volunteered to lead the way. You see—you are not the only one who has made alternate plans."

Neil looked startled. "I was going to send Durward's lieutenant. After all, he knows the land well. Atholl is an old man, and ailing."

"Then he is of little use to you," Elizabeth answered, her voice low and sensible. "Besides, he knows the country well enough, having visited here often."

"Elizabeth, I will not allow—" he began.

She stopped him with a queen's look and withdrew her hand. "Enough, dear Neil. We do not have time to argue. You will need all the soldiers here with you. We will either escape by stealth or be found. And if we are found, it will not matter how many men we have with us for they will not be enough."

I drew in an audible breath. Aunts Mary and Christina took hands. But Uncle Neil gave in with a sigh of resignation.

Just then Atholl appeared leading his horse behind him. He looked much better for a good night's sleep in a proper bed, and his white beard was newly clean, but he was still pale, and his cough—if anything—was worse, having moved deep down into his chest.

"I will go on ahead—*cough, cough*—to make certain all is safe," he said, nodding toward the little gate that was to be our exit. "They—*cough*—call that drop out there the back den. It leads to—*cough, cough*—a small stream, and once we're across that, we can be away." He bowed once to Elizabeth and passed through the doorway, though not before having to stop and bend over with a spasm of coughing.

I suddenly found myself trembling until Uncle Neil enfolded me in a farewell embrace, his long arms wrapped around me. Then he took off his right gauntlet and plucked the silver thistle ring from his finger and offered it to me.

"It was a gift from my father, your grandfather," he said. "I wear it always for luck. You take it now and it will guard you on your journey."

I drew myself up and spoke with the same quiet dignity Elizabeth had just shown him. "No, thank you, Uncle Neil. We have my father's ring for safe passage," I told him. "Besides, I want *you* to have all the luck in the world."

We made the rest of our good-byes and left Kildrummy, sneaking out the back way, not like the royal family of Scotland, but like thieves stealing the Kildrummy silver. The only ones who waved us on were the servants. The soldiers were all at their posts and the knights, with Uncle Neil, already on their horses and away.

The slope down to where the horses waited was steep and slick and I would have lost my footing more than once if Isabel had not grabbed hold of me at crucial moments. At each slip I felt a fool.

Three men—the cook, blacksmith, and castle carpenter— were waiting by the stream with our horses, who looked rested and ready for the new journey. They helped us mount up, and then John of Atholl led us north.

I took one final look back at Kildrummy rising grey and stony behind us. Then I made a silent prayer that God keep my dear uncle Neil and all the others within it safe.

But under my breast, right against the bone, I had a strange pain that would not go away, as if my heart guessed what my head did not. I looked at the others, so stern-faced on their horses, and wondered if they felt the same. Still, I dared not speak the fear aloud lest I make it so.

24 ❧ THE ELEVENTH DAY OF MY CAPTIVITY

I wake after another full night's sleep. In fact, I have slept so well, the monk—my royal chaplain—has already delivered my breakfast porridge. It is already cold. Thank goodness this is no longer summer as it would likely have been covered with flies.

I sit cross-legged, with the bowl in my lap. With the spoon I pick at the porridge. It seems a bit thicker than usual. Is there some meaning here? I am like an old priest in the Bible, reading the entrails of a sacrifice: a bullock, a lamb.

Lamb. I must not think of lamb. Or rabbit. Or venison. I must not think of grapes or blackberries or honey. I must not remember my last breakfast in Kildrummy—two duck eggs. There is a strange growling in my stomach. I must not think about duck eggs. I will go mad with hunger if I do.

As I worry myself this way, cross-legged in the middle of the cage, three boys come by, and I watch them out of the corner of my eye.

Are they the rat boys?

They keep their distance and stare curiously at me. They elbow one another and pick at scabs on their arms. The October sun is at their backs, slanted, and their faces are in shadow. I am disturbed by their attention and certain I have seen them before among the stone throwers. Among the tatties and neep throwers.

But not the rat boys.

No.

At supper my monk comes again with the ration of gruel. This time it is lukewarm and lumpy, which is at least a change. Without prompting, my monk perches on the narrow ledge as if afraid it will give way under his weight.

I tell him about the beautiful mirror Father gave me one birthday, along with a caution about vanity. Thinking of Father brings hot tears to my eyes.

The monk's mouth twitches, stretches, smiles. He smiles! Not at my tears, but because of my talk of vanity. Emboldened by this, I tell him about all the fine things we had to eat that day.

"Not that I am complaining about the food I get here," I am quick to add, knocking the wooden spoon against the wooden bowl. "Certainly I am being well taken care of—for a prisoner."

He blinks once, twice, his smile gone. Perhaps he is thinking about how other women prisoners are treated—if there are others. He bites his lower lip.

The guard outside the priory has been keeping a close eye on us, looking once or twice as if he is ready to leave his position and come toward us, but then thinks better of it.

My chaplain does not notice the guard. His eyes are fixed on his beads, running them through his fingers.

But he is thinking. I can almost hear him.

By now I can no longer pretend there is anything left in my cup or my bowl. I surrender them to him. Surprisingly, he reaches into his cassock and, hunching his shoulders to hide his movement from the guard, pulls out a book.

A book!

I can scarce credit it.

He hands it to me and I take it, quickly slipping it under my skirt. The skirt that was once a lovely green and is now a nasty grey.

Then I watch as the monk returns to the priory under the frowning gaze of the guard.

I wait till the guard has gone for his own meal, and slip the book out again. Settling into a corner of the cage, I sit down and, bending over with the book in my lap. I do my best to look as though I have just dozed off. Anyone watching me will not wonder what I am up to.

I read the words copied out in pen and ink by some studious monk. It is a life of a local saint called Cuthbert. I have never heard of him, but according to the book he was very famous in these parts. He lived alone on an island for many years. Then, one day, when he least expected it, God called him back to the mainland, where he became a bishop.

Not much of a life, I think. He was never chased across Scotland by soldiers. He was never put in a cage. I envy him his quiet sainthood.

I wonder if my monk intends this book to be a message. If so, what can it be telling me? That, one day, when I am not counting on it, God will send someone to rescue me? That Father or Uncle Neil or even good old Atholl will find me?

Or perhaps this slender volume is the only one the monk could find.

At last I decide it does not matter. A book is a wonderful present. Better than a mirror, I think. Though it may grow worn, it will never grow old.

Besides, now I have a chaplain, a lady to wait upon me—and a royal library.

The rest is sure to follow.

It is evening and I am sitting in the far corner of the cage toying with the cord that binds my dress at the waist. The book is safely hidden in my small clothes, under the filthy gown.

As I toy with the cord, I remember other cords and belts I have worn. I see them with my mind's eye. A cincture of golden flowers I wore to Father and Elizabeth's wedding. A belt with a silver buckle cunningly shaped like a thistle, which Uncle Neil had made for me in London.

It is a memory game to keep myself occupied, and it works. I do not notice Longshanks until he clears his throat. I look up, almost guiltily. His chest is thrust out like a rooster's, which surprises me. As usual, he has sent his escort away.

"Have you noticed how my health is improved?" he asks.

It is true. There is a slight flush to his cheeks that was not there before. His eyes seem clearer. Still, I wonder why he tells me this, speaking so familiarly, as if we are friends. I need to be on guard. Longshanks does not say things without a reason.

"My physicians prescribed herbal baths and pomegranate wine."

I say nothing.

He smiles, as if he takes my silence as agreement or approval. I do not like it when he smiles. His smile reminds me of an adder's. He keeps talking, his hand resting lightly on one of the bars of the cage. "Normally I think them ignorant imposters but for once their remedies appear to have worked. I have not felt so well in months."

Still I say nothing but his mood is so hearty, my silence does not seem to prick him as it did before. Indeed, I feel a forboding and stop myself from shivering.

"The news from Scotland," he says jauntily, "serves my humors even better."

Surely my cheeks have gone pale, for they are suddenly cold as if touched by a north wind.

"The whole country is in my grasp," he says in that same cheery voice. "Your father darts from one rat hole to another."

I want to snap at him, like a caged beast. But I hold my tongue. Silence, I remind myself. Silence will be my weapon.

"What, no defense of King Hob today? Has your tongue frozen in the night?" His voice has begun to lose some of its good humor.

So I am right. He needs me to rise to his taunts. His victory over Scotland is not complete without this.

But has he a victory? Or is he just bluffing? He says Father hides in one rat hole or another.

I think: If Father is hiding, then he is not caught.

A rat not caught may still devour the cheese.

I look down at the cord once more and force Longshanks from my mind. I count it like a rosary and even hum a little.

Longshanks circles the cage, trying to catch my eye. "You look well enough under the circumstances," he observes. "I see it is not a cold nor a fever that has brought you to this state of lassitude. So I have to assume you are doing this on purpose."

My back is getting sore and I shift a bit, stretching my shoulders, but do not look up.

Longshanks takes this as an acknowledgment.

"You do not stand in the presence of the king?" he asks. Now his voice takes on an edge. "Perhaps your legs have grown weak from lack of exercise. You should get up and walk around more. You see how I walk even though my legs pain me. I will not be ruled by infirmity . . ."—he stops his circuit of the cage and draws closer to the bars—"any more than I will be crossed by an underage rebel."

I toss the ends of the belt up and down before me.

His voice rises and he sounds like a petulant child. "Have you nothing to ask me? Do you not want to know where your father was last heard of?"

How stupid he is. Of course I want to know. But I will not ask. To ask is to lose the battle.

"This is insolence!" he roars. "I command you to speak!"

Still looking down at the cord, I smile as if to say: "You are not my king to command anything from me." He knows what I am thinking but he can not make me say it aloud.

There comes a harsh outbreak of coughing. I can imagine his face turning purple as the spasm shakes his body. Atholl shook that way and turned that very color on the last days before we were taken.

"Away!" I hear him croak angrily. I know the words are directed at his attendant, who is surely rushing to his master's aid.

At last the coughing dies away. Longshanks' breathing is normal again. I tell myself not to look up and see how he is doing, and I do not, but it is hard.

Finally Longshanks speaks in a serpent's voice, hissing with pleasure. "See, I have something here to interest you."

I do not look at him, though the cord game has outlasted its usefulness. Instead I now think of other things from happier times. The view from my window at Lochmaben. Greeting Father after he has been gone a long time in England. Dancing with Uncle Neil in the Great Hall. Riding my pony with my falcon, Ranger, on my arm, her claws caught tight in the leather of my glove.

I will think of anything, so long as it guards me against Longshanks' snake voice.

A new sound interrupts my memories.

Clink . . . clink . . . clink.

It is a strange sound, and alien. I force myself to sit still and not turn.

Longshanks is tapping something metallic against one of the bars of the cage.

Clink . . . clink . . . clink.

Is it the key to my prison?

Does he mean to let me out at last?

I think longingly of a bed, a bath, a real meal with a knife into meat.

No—such thoughts will trap me. I will not . . .

Clink . . . clink . . . clink.

"I am certain you will want to see this," he hisses.

The tapping continues, now louder and more urgent.

Clink . . . clink . . . clink.

I cannot help myself. I look over and then I gasp at what he holds between his thumb and forefinger, what he has been hitting against the bar: a ring, a silver ring decorated with a thistle.

There is a cold grin on his face.

"Do you recognize it?" he asks.

I can do nothing to keep my lips from parting. They speak on their own without my willing.

"Yes," I say, "it belongs to Uncle Neil."

He nods. In victory he is almost gracious, almost gentle.

Now that I have spoken, I have to continue. "How have you come by it?" Though I am afraid to know.

"We took Kildrummy," he said.

I draw in a deep breath.

He cannot help but gloat. "Where siege weapons did not work, traitor's gold did."

When I do not ask who the traitor was, he tells me, but I might have guessed.

"There was one still loyal to his king in the castle, and a bit of a bribe brought him home. He set fire to the grain in the hall and it quickly spread. A man well versed in flames, our Osbourne; his smithy trained him well." Longshanks laughs and the mask of gentleness is dropped. He holds the ring out to me. "I thought you would like to have it."

"Give it back to Neil Bruce, for it was his father's," I say.

"You do not yet understand," Longshanks says coldly. "Neil Bruce has no more use for it."

For a long moment I stare at the ring, conjuring up Uncle Neil's handsome face as I last saw it. His handsome, honorable, loving face.

Do not tell me, I pray. Do not say the words.

But Longshanks keeps nothing back. He crowds into the bars of the cage. His face is so close to mine, I can smell the sourness of his breath. He stinks of death. "I had Neil Bruce hanged, drawn, and quartered, a fit punishment for treason. His head now sits on a spike over the gate of Berwick Castle."

I grab the ring from his hand and then I start to shake, as if I am the old, palsied one and Longshanks the child. I clasp my hands together but still they shake. There is a cold spot under my breastbone. I cannot breathe.

I will kill you, old man, I think. I will have you tortured and hanged and set your head on my bedpost that I may watch the flesh as it drops from the bones. I will spit on your skull and spread sheep droppings on it.

As I think this, I begin to breathe again. Then I put the end of the cord through the ring and tie it tightly. At last I glance down at the ring, remembering how Uncle Neil looked when he offered it to me.

For luck.

After a minute or an hour or a day of my silence, Long-shanks walks away.

And then—only then—do I weep.

25 ❧ TAIN, NORTHERN SCOTLAND, OCTOBER 1306

I had never traveled so far north before. The country grew wilder and strangely more beautiful the farther we rode. It was not the beauty of rolling hills and soft carpets of flowers that I was used to, but of rugged mountain heights and thick purple heather.

Yet who could enjoy such stark beauty when fear rode behind us every step of the way.

Twice we had to hide in gullies when Atholl thought there were enemy scouts about. We had to bind the horses' muzzles with cloth to keep them from whickering.

Crouching down under gorse, I was pricked cruelly by the thorns but did not dare complain.

Suddenly I saw movement in the trail above us.

Friend or foe?

I glanced over at Atholl, who raised a finger against his lips, signaling me that we did not dare break cover to find out.

At night we slept without a warming fire for fear of giving away our position. Every one of us caught a chill. Aunt Christina began to cough as much as Atholl, and my nose started running like a river in flood.

After three days of this, our brief sojourn at Kildrummy seemed but a passing dream.

At one short stop I asked Elizabeth, "Will we always be running like this?"

She reached out and touched my hair. "I must find a comb." It was no answer at all.

We approached the coastal town of Tain, which was no more than a cluster of cottages huddled around a grey, granite church as if they could be warmed by it.

Atholl assured us—between spasms of coughing—that there would be a boat there waiting to take us to Orkney.

"But we must tread carefully," he warned. "This territory belongs to Earl William of Ross."

"Is he an enemy, too?" I asked.

Atholl shook his head, his watery eyes sad. "There is no real wickedness in the man, but he clings foolishly to John Balliol as his king."

"Toom Tabard," Isabel said bitterly. Her lovely face was now so sun burned, it was almost as red as her hair.

Aunts Mary and Christina mouthed the nickname together, "Toom Tabard . . ." And Christina added, "We have enemies everywhere."

Elizabeth heard her and, drawing herself up in the saddle, said, "Ladies—we must have courage!"

And, suddenly, somehow, we did.

We were on the road to the harbor and I could hear the grey northern sea pounding like a drumbeat against the rocky shore. It sounded as if it were calling to me: *Come away. Come away.* But where would it take me? Away from everything I knew and loved. Away from Scotland and Father and the uncles and Lochmaben. Away from Maggie and my hawk, Ranger, and . . .

"Ho there!" Isabel exclaimed. "Is that trouble ahead?"

A group of armed men were loitering about a hundred yards up the roadside, without a banner or tabard to identify them. I counted a dozen. They were rough-looking, bearded, in dark-green jerkins.

Elizabeth made a sound against her teeth and the aunts drew in loud, ragged breaths.

The men moved briskly to block our path to Tain.

"Are they Ross' men?" Elizabeth asked.

"As like as not," Atholl replied grimly. "But they might let us pass if we do nought to enflame them."

We rode forward trying to do as he said, nodding at them and waving. But my heart was beating so loudly, I wondered it did not drown out the sound of the sea.

The leader of the armed band walked toward us, his hand upraised. A man of Uncle Neil's age, he had a squared-off face that looked as if it had been carved out of wood, each curl of his beard a wood shaving.

"What business have you here?" His voice was as rough as his clothing.

Atholl reined in his horse, as did we all. "Have the times grown so wicked that innocent travelers cannot pass in peace?"

"These are times of treachery and rebellion," the man answered, reaching for Atholl's reins, but the old man was alert to that trick and backed away.

"Our *business* is honest," Atholl said firmly. "Step aside and let us pass. I accompany these women and they—as you can see—are neither treacherous nor rebellious."

The man made no move to comply but squinted hard at Atholl's face. "I know you, do I not? John, Earl of Atholl?"

"I am, and that is all the more reason why you should not detain me," Atholl replied firmly.

"You have been following the usurper, Robert Bruce?"

The hush that greeted the question was like the calm before a great blow.

At last Atholl answered, "I have been serving my country in good conscience. Can you say the same?"

The man turned his gaze toward the rest of us. "And who might these fine ladies be?"

I almost laughed. *Fine ladies indeed!* We were filthy, ragged, and exhausted. Any fool could see that. But I was too frightened to do more than wipe my runny nose on my sleeve.

"These ladies are under my protection," Atholl responded. "That is all the answer you need." He waved a hand at the man. "Now let us pass."

For a moment, the authority and confidence in Atholl's voice seemed to give the leader of the pack pause. He looked back at his guards, then back at us, weighing the odds.

What odds? I thought. *Four women, a girl, and one sick old man?*

Stroking his wood-shavings beard thoughtfully, the man then said, "Let me accompany you to my master, the Earl of Ross, so that he might speak with you."

That, of course, was the very last thing we wanted to do.

"We have tarried long enough," Atholl replied, letting his voice show impatience. "Now give ground!" He drew his sword in a motion so quick, the man took a pace backward. *Old* Atholl might be, but he was still a force to be reckoned with.

Shrinking into the ranks of his followers, the man spoke in quick whispers, too soft for us to hear. One of the guards was sent dashing toward the town while the others raised their spears and swords, presenting us with a wall of steel.

This does not look good, I thought, once more wiping my streaming nose.

Atholl turned in his saddle and said to Elizabeth and me, "That is a messenger running for William of Ross, I would guess. The rest are more than enough to hold us from the town until he arrives."

Isabel rode up to us. "Surely we cannot just wait here and be gathered up like hens for the slaughter."

Aunts Mary and Christina came as well. They looked both startled and concerned, a lot like the hens Isabel spoke of. "What should we do?" they said, their hands waving about. "Where can we go?"

"We *dare* not wait," Elizabeth decided. "John?"

He stroked his beard in thought, then said, "The road to the boat is closed to us, but off to the east, across this meadow, is a shrine to St. Duthac. Anyone who claims the saint's protection should be granted sanctuary there by the laws of the church."

"Then," said Elizabeth, wheeling Caledonia about, "if no one else will help us, we will recruit the saint to our cause. And to Scotland's."

The men on the road barked at us to stop, but they were on foot and so were too slow to give chase. Their angry voices faded behind us, as did the sound of the sea.

We rode swiftly across the meadow, with gulls screaming above us. Ahead, almost hidden in a dip, was a small stone chapel.

"St. Duthac's shrine!" Atholl cried, pointing with his right hand.

We urged the horses onward.

The sinking sun thrust our shadows toward the chapel like fingers grasping for safety.

As I held tight to Elizabeth's waist, I tried to pray and failed. What I wanted was suddenly simple: to be inside the shrine and protected by the stones. And by God.

At the sound of our hoofbeats two startled monks rushed out of the shrine and signaled to us to stop. I think they feared we would ride right into the chapel.

We pulled the horses to a halt and Elizabeth dismounted first. "Good brothers," she cried, "we claim sanctuary of this shrine."

"From whom?" one of the monks asked. He had a wandering eye, which kept glancing up the road. I had the oddest feeling that the eye was expecting an entire army to come flooding over the horizon.

"Does it matter?" Elizabeth asked. "Is sanctuary not available to any Christian who claims it?"

"Of course it is," the other monk replied. He smiled, but it was a wolf's smile, not a shepherd's. "Understand, my lady, we cannot involve ourselves in—"

"You need not involve yourselves in *anything*," Elizabeth said, waving them aside. "Just let us in. And take care of these horses of ours. They are innocent of any sin or crime so you may attend them without disturbing your scruples."

We were all off our horses by then. Isabel came close and whispered in my ear, "*That* is a queen worth following, my girl!"

Once we were inside the candle-lit chapel, Atholl slumped down on the nearest stone bench, his head sunk down on his chest, his white beard tufted out like a bird's nest. He started to cough, wiping his sleeve across his mouth. When the spasm passed at last, he looked up at Elizabeth.

"Ross is no fool," he said, his voice harsh from coughing. "He will find us soon enough."

"Yes," Elizabeth agreed, "but this is a house of God. By the laws of sanctuary, he cannot lay hands on us here. At the very least, we will have gained some time."

For a moment, I felt a great sense of relief. I looked up at the aunts—who had come over to me—and smiled.

Aunt Mary smiled back, but Aunt Christina was shaking her head vigorously.

"What use is sanctuary?" she said in a dismal voice. "Our doom follows us like a hound on the scent."

"But we are safe here, surely," Aunt Mary said reassuringly.

I wanted to agree, but suddenly I remembered that Red Comyn had been struck down in church by Father. *What sanctuary had that been?* My face felt hot, then cold, and I collapsed on one of the stone benches.

Aunt Christina had not finished her litany yet. "In the end we will be taken by force or starved into submission."

Holding a finger to her lips, Aunt Mary shushed her. "You are frightening the child."

I sat up straight. "I am *not* a child," I said. "Not any longer."

But Aunt Christina was now in full cry, her eyes wild and staring. "My husband may be captured or dead already," she moaned, "so why should I prolong an empty life?" With a surprising move, she pulled something from the folds of her skirt.

For a moment, in the flickering candlelight, I was not certain what she held. But when she held a knife to her breast, we were all shocked, none more so than Aunt Mary, who gasped and put a hand over her mouth.

"Would it not be best," Aunt Christina said, the hand holding the knife shaking, "to put an end to ourselves and deny Longshanks his prize? We will be martyrs to the cause. It would put steel in Robert and his followers and . . ."

My limbs had gone suddenly like ice. I could not move. Aunt Mary was equally still.

But Elizabeth came toward us. Taking careful steps and speaking to Aunt Christina as she would a wild animal, Elizabeth said calmly, "Christina, dear Christina, it is only weariness and despair that makes you speak thus, not courage." Her voice was firm. "Our lives are given to us by God and only He will decree when they are to be taken away. If He has preserved us this far, He must have a purpose in mind. What that purpose is we cannot guess." With gentle force she coaxed the dagger from my aunt's trembling fingers and dropped it on the floor. At that, the steel went out of Aunt Christina and she collapsed weeping.

All at once my limbs unfroze. I stood and went to Aunt Christina and put my arms around her, but Isabel knelt and picked up the dagger. "Is it not better, Christina, to turn our blades against our enemies, just as our menfolk would? If we are to be taken, let them pay a price in blood."

Elizabeth glared at her. "They could kill us all easily," she said sharply. "And you would give them reason to, with your foolish bravado. We are not warriors, and I will not have us throw our lives away playing at knights. Not while there is so much at stake."

Isabel looked angry at first, then abashed. Once the first heat of emotion had ebbed, she could see the sanity of Elizabeth's words.

Elizabeth turned, and as if speaking only to herself, said,

"Sometimes it is easier to die than to live. But our duty is to live, to breathe." She paused. "To hope."

"And to win in the end," I whispered.

"Aye," Isabel echoed, "to win in the end."

Atholl stood up and moved to one of the lancet windows, his age dropping away from him in an instant. "Ross is here," he announced, unsheathing his sword.

Sir," cried one of the monks, coming over to him and placing a hand on Atholl's arm, "this is a house of God. Do not let your steel free here."

Atholl shook him off.

"Brother," he said, "there comes the dragon. Would you have me let these ladies be set on fire because of a bit of altar and stone?" His voice echoed off the walls like a great bell.

We crowded around him and through the window saw a small band of horsemen approaching from the west followed by a long line of foot soldiers.

Aunt Christina laughed. There was a tinge of hysteria in it. "That dragon has many teeth, old man. Do you think you can pull them all?" She was quieted only when Aunt Mary put an arm around her.

"*Will* Ross respect the law of sanctuary?" Elizabeth asked urgently. I stood by her shoulder as if her courage could rub off on me.

Wearily, Atholl shook his head. "I suspect he would rather we surrendered ourselves. That way he can avoid the taint of sacrilege. But take us he will. We are his proof of loyalty to Edward Longshanks. He will not pass up an opportunity to play the loyal dog."

"Then can I buy us time by negotiating with him?" Elizabeth pressed him.

"What purpose will that serve?" Isabel spoke and drew out her own short sword from its sheath. She held it up and looked as fierce as a warrior queen.

What purpose indeed?

I thought about all that had gone before, the frantic race north and west. The plans to sail to Norway. I was finally beginning to understand. Elizabeth and Atholl were not protecting the aunts or Isabel or themselves. This whole dash to safety had been for my sake. Father was king, and I his sole heir. If Father is killed, I would be queen after him. So it was *I* who imperiled all.

I gasped aloud.

Elizabeth seemed to know my thoughts. She put her arms around me and drew me close, saying over my head to Isabel, "The *purpose* is for you to sneak Marjorie out the back of the chapel. With God's help, the two of you will make your way unseen to the ship that waits to take you to Orkney."

"Think what you are asking," Aunt Mary warned. Her normally placid face was pinched with fear.

"I have given it *much* thought," Elizabeth said. "Perhaps I can dazzle Ross for long enough that they may escape. I am a rich prize, but Marjorie is richer still, for she is Robert's—"

I drew away from her. "I am Father's heir," I said. I gazed into Aunt Mary's eyes. "His sole heir." Then I turned, almost apologetically, to Elizabeth. "I do not say that to hurt you."

She smiled a bit wanly, the shadows around her face emphasizing her bones. For a moment she looked as beautiful as a saint. "Robert can always marry again, child, but *you* are irreplaceable."

I ran to her and threw my arms around her waist, suddenly frightened. "I know if I leave I will never see Scotland again."

Elizabeth petted my hair and there was a catch in her voice when she spoke. "Be strong. Be your father's daughter. You are his only legitimate hope for continuing his line. It is from you that the future kings of Scotland will spring."

"Come," said Isabel, handing me the dagger. "We will be women warriors together. Our turn to fight will come another day. Look—here is the small door at the back and there should be only a short distance till we are under the cover of the trees. No one will see us leave if we go now."

Reluctantly, I started toward the door with Isabel. Then I turned and looked into the church. In the flickering light I took in Atholl standing by the window, sword in hand. My aunts, side by side, arms entwined, watching me. Elizabeth . . . Elizabeth was weeping.

It was another parting. I wanted no more of them.

"No," I said, turning back. "If I am truly a princess of Scotland, then I will *not* abandon my country. And I will *not* abandon you."

As I watched, Elizabeth's face changed. First her eyes widened in shock, her mouth and jaw went rigid with fear and horror, then they softened with resignation and understanding. Finally, wordlessly, she stretched out her arms to me.

I ran over and she wrapped her arms around me in a tight embrace.

"Stay, then," she breathed into my hair. "And God help us all."

Just then there was an uproar of voices from outside, like waves battering the shore.

"They have dragged some monks from hiding," Atholl reported from the window. "Now here comes Ross, that doughty bastard. As red in temper as in hair."

Leaving the window, he quickly found a couple of wooden chairs and set them against the door. They did not look as though they would stand much battering.

In a firm voice, but one laced with urgency, he said, "Go to the altar, ladies. Run, run. It will be safest there."

We had scarcely gotten across the small room when the chapel door crashed open, shattering both the chairs at once.

A pair of soldiers crossed the threshold, their swords before them.

Elizabeth grabbed my hand and pulled me behind her. The aunts stood on either side. Short sword upraised, Isabel stood on the altar step. She looked every inch an avenging angel, her red hair frizzed about her head like a halo.

The next man who came through the door had a wild orange beard. His sword was still in its sheath. I knew by his bearing that he had to be Earl William of Ross.

Elizabeth released her hold on me and advanced to meet him as boldly as if she were at the head of an army. Straightening her weather-stained skirts and lifting her chin proudly, she warned him, "You are in violation of sanctuary, sir. God does not take such things lightly."

"You must be Robert Bruce's bride," said Ross. "I heard you had spirit."

"Spirit enough to be queen," said Elizabeth.

"And spirit enough," he said, "to be no easy prisoner, I guess."

"I will not be a prisoner lest you violate this holy shrine." She stared him down.

"Madam," he said, spreading his large hands before him as a sign of his sincerity, "I do not wish to violate anything. Leastwise this shrine if I can avoid it. But you *must* come with me. I promise that you will in no way be ill-treated." He tried a smile. He was not good at it.

"We are no brigands or traitors to be handed over to our English foes," she said. "And in fact, sir, we are on our way out of the country where we cannot trouble you more. What spite against us drives you to stop us? Surely our exile will only *help* your cause, not hinder it."

Huzzah, Elizabeth! I thought. I wondered how Ross would answer that!

He bowed his head to her, not as a queen but as an equal. "I have no quarrel with *you*, madam, and you make good sense. However, my loyalty to King John Balliol demands that I make you my prisoners."

"John Balliol? That Toom Tabard?" Elizabeth's voice was full of disdain. "What manner of man are you that you would rather serve an empty coat than a true king who even now fights to set your country free?"

For a moment something like a cloud passed across his face. Her words seemed to make him uneasy. Then he shook himself like an old dog just out of a cold bath. "Your husband's cause is lost, madam," he said with passion, "and only a fool would fight on for him now."

I could see his answer infuriated her, but she did not lose possession of herself. Instead, in a quiet voice, and leaning forward so that they were almost nose to nose, she said, "But if against all odds he should yet prove victorious?"

He leaned away from her and shrugged, saying as softly, "Then we would be in the presence of a miracle."

She moved even closer. It was as if they were now the best of friends. "As a Christian, do you *not* believe in miracles?"

Ross looked a bit alarmed. "As a Christian, madam, I *do* believe in miracles, but as a Scotsman I do not look for them." He folded his arms over his chest. I think he did it to keep her at bay.

"Then you are a poor Christian and an even poorer Scotsman," she told him. Her back was now straight as if there were a rod of steel there.

I wondered at her strength. And wondered more at what game she was playing with him.

She continued, "But swear to me now that if such a miracle should occur, then you will accept it as a sign that God Himself has chosen Robert as your rightful king."

I leaned forward to hear his answer.

He flapped his hands at her as one would a goose. "*Pah!* This is empty talk."

She did not stand down. "Not so empty unless a man be too mean to listen to it. Make me that promise and I swear we shall give ourselves up willingly and you need not take us in defiance of God and His church."

Aha! I understood it now. She had trapped him and he was looking for a way out. So battles could be fought without swords. It was a useful thing to know.

Ross shook his head angrily. "Woman, you tire me. I can simply take you now without such an oath."

"Swear it."

I held my breath. Could she win this war of wits? And if so, what would she win? Would we not still be prisoners?

Elizabeth said simply, "Is it better to commit a sin than to swear an oath?"

Ross took a deep breath. "Very well. If only to avoid desecration of this holy place."

Now it was Elizabeth who folded her arms before her, like a tutor with a balking student.

He shook his head. "I do swear as you ask, madam. If Robert Bruce—against all odds—wins through, he shall be my king. I vow this on the saint's altar. Are you satisfied now?"

"I am," she said, holding her hands up in a gesture of submission. "Then we are yours."

But her concession suddenly sounded to me like victory and not defeat.

So we were made prisoners and put in wagons and surrounded by Ross' men so that there was no chance to escape. Besides, we had been made fast by Elizabeth's promise.

While riding in a wagon was more comfortable than riding double on our poor horse, we could not—of course—go where we willed.

As we traveled south, I realized how much of Scotland seemed to be in English hands. We no longer went on the back roads and on dirt tracks, over the deer trails and through deep wooded glens. Now we followed the main highway. Everywhere were English banners, and people—Scots people—jeered as our carts rolled by.

Aunts Mary and Christina seemed almost content that we were prisoners, for at least this way they knew what to expect. Elizabeth kept her own counsel, as did Atholl. But Isabel seemed to sicken with each passing mile, as if captivity were a dagger in her heart.

As for me, I did not know what to think. I was Father's heir and so I needed to be brave. But all I really wanted was a hot bath and clean clothes.

If, I thought, we had to sit out the rest of the war in a prison, how was that worse than hiding in the heather and gorse, sleeping rough, and eating nettle soup? Either way, once Father had won, all would be well.

Did we no longer need courage? That I didn't know. But what I didn't guess was that this was to be the beginning of a deeper, stranger war than anything that had gone before.

At Stirling, that great stone fortress overlooking the River Forth, Ross' men handed us over to a squad of English soldiers.

"Here," he said to them abruptly. *Washing his hands of us like Pontius Pilate,* I thought. "May you have a better time with them than I."

The soldiers seemed rough, but they were also silent all the way to Berwick on the very border of England.

It surprised me that the countryside we passed through was pleasant, with blossoming fall flowers whose names I knew: foxglove and campion, hedge bindweed and rose bay. I had expected everything to be wilting and sere. At the very least, here on the border of Scotland, nature should have been in mourning for us.

Was I being foolish? I suppose so. But I had never fought a war before, never been taken off to prison before. I think I wanted great drama. What I got were small miseries and a pretty landscape.

Our escort split into several parties at Berwick. Each group took a different captive on a different road.

I tried to cling to Elizabeth but we were pulled roughly apart and I was bundled onto a dirty farm cart.

Elizabeth kissed her palm and blew the parting kiss toward me. Standing in the midst of her enemies, she looked every inch the queen.

I stretched out my hands toward her as the wagon drove away, but a soldier grabbed me by the shoulder and yanked me back.

"Mother!" I cried. And then my throat seemed to close and I could not say a word more.

She looked at me with a tenderness and strength.

Then she was gone.

The soldiers seemed embarrassed so many of them should be needed to guard one small girl.

I suppose they would have been happier chasing through the Highlands after my father and uncles and the few who follow them. But instead the Englishmen had to keep an eye on me.

On me.

Marjorie Bruce.

The Scottish king's only daughter.

I vowed on my dead mother's name, and my living mother's, that they would some day pay for it.

And so would their wicked king.

27 ❧ THE TWELFTH DAY OF MY CAPTIVITY

My round-faced chaplain comes with my morning watery gruel, but I do not have the heart for my usual chatter. I lean against the bars of my cage and scarcely touch the food.

He seems to understand, and sits for a while with me, which is a comfort.

"Uncle Neil," I say suddenly. A tear slides down the side of my nose. I can say nothing more; my tongue sticks to the roof of my mouth. I am afraid if it loosens, all that will come out will be sobs.

Just then two men come striding down from the priory. One is a guard whom I have seen before. His face is a purposeful blank, as if he holds his character away from his features. The other is a lean man with silver hair, flyaway silver eyebrows, and an air of easy authority. I expect he is captain of the guard.

At the sight of them, the monk leaps to his feet so suddenly he almost falls over.

"You know the king's orders," the captain barks at him. "No one is to talk to the prisoner."

"I d-d-did not t-talk," stammers the monk. It is very odd to hear his voice. I wonder if he always stammers or if it is because he is afraid.

"You are not to keep company with her either," the captain snaps. "Fetch her food, clean out the privy. Other than that, keep clear of her."

In all this, the guard is silent and I wonder that he is there at all. Perhaps he wonders, too.

The monk's head bobs obediently and he scurries off so quickly, he almost trips over his robe.

I want to shout at the captain for being so unkind, but fear that if I do so I might only make more trouble for the monk.

"You keep a close eye and be sure nobody else comes near her," the captain tells the guard. Then he stamps away, a satisfied look on his face.

The guard stands at attention. He does not look happy to be guarding a filthy girl who is hardly a threat, locked away in cage.

I fall asleep in midmorning. When I wake the first time, I see the guard has been replaced by another. He has been given no direct orders to stand over me and so has retreated to the shelter of the gate. I see him chatting with a friend.

The day goes by slowly. A light rain falls and the patter on the roof of the cage soothes me back into sleep again. Perhaps I am fevered. Perhaps I am sick at heart.

I sleep, wake, sleep again. My thoughts are full of Uncle Neil. Alive—not dead. I do not dare think of him dead, his wonderful eyes being pecked out by crows.

Another time I wake, and it is night. The rain has stopped and the guards are off somewhere. Perhaps they are drinking together. Father often had to punish guards at Lochmaben who whiled away the nights drinking with friends.

That makes me think of Father. I wonder if he has heard

that we have been captured. If so, he will be suffering. I do not want him to suffer. He cannot fight properly if he is suffering.

I wonder if he knows about Uncle Neil.

Suddenly I sit bolt upright. Longshanks taxed me with Uncle Neil's awful death, but he has said nothing of Father. He would never be able to keep such a death secret.

So this one thing I know. This one bit of comfort. Uncle Neil may be dead and we women in cages. But Father lives. And with him, Scotland lives. If I remember nothing else, I must remember this: Scotland lives!

I start to fall asleep again when I hear a hushed whisper of voices approaching from the direction of the village. I count the crouched shapes creeping toward me through the darkness. I make out five of them.

A sudden panic clutches my belly. Could these be mischief makers, rat catchers, even murderers sent by the captain of the guard?

For a second I think I see Uncle Neil's head on its pike. My belly grows cold. My hand goes to my neck. Then I shrink away into a far corner of the cage.

"Princess," whispers a familiar voice. "It's me. Enid."

I am so relieved, I almost let out a cheer, but I do not.

"Who are these others, Lady Enid?" I ask. I try to sound welcoming rather than suspicious.

My use of her title turns out to be just the right touch. She comes close. "This be my sister Ruth. That be Mark, our brother. And these be cousins, Toby and Jacob."

I peer at the shadows and make out a girl about a year older than Enid with the same oval face, only a little rounder about the bosom. I recognize the boys as the three I had seen passing by earlier. The younger two are snotty-nosed, but the older one is almost a man. This close they smell.

I expect I smell, too.

"I be telling them all about ye and how yer to become a queen and how I be one of your ladies." Enid grins at me. Even in the shadows I can make out her mossy teeth.

"You are all welcome," I say, "for a queen needs a court, even if it is only in a courtyard."

They laugh quietly at my little joke and squat down on the ground on the opposite side from the gate. Obviously they are cautious. And I imagine they know a lot about being sly. They will need those skills if they are to serve me.

Enid tries to perform a sort of curtsy, but it is not easy in that position. "We be glad of being here," she says.

"Ye think ye be some sort of queen then?" says Mark, the brother, who is the tallest and oldest of the boys. He has a round head, like a bread roll, and flaxen hair. He sounds skeptical. I understand then that to convince them all I must first convince him.

"I am a princess," I say plainly. "But since my father, King Robert, is not here, I will have to rule in his place." I spread my hands to indicate the cage that surrounds me.

Mark looks at the two younger boys. "She be barking mad," he sneers. "All that time in a cage, I mind."

"Mark, ye promised to be nice," Ruth reproaches him. She turns to me. "I'd be a lady, too," she says, "just like Enid."

"And so you shall be, Lady Ruth," I tell her, "though my palace is a humble one."

Ruth beams. I can tell because the shadow now has teeth that shine in the moonlight. The moonlight also highlights her tangled hair. Though it is no more tangled, I fear, than mine. "Oh, that canna be helped."

"Not for the present," I agree.

"Well, we ain't ladies and we ain't servants," says Jacob. He slashes the back of his hand under his snotty nose.

"I need no servants," I say quickly. "What I do need are knights."

"Knights?" Mark's mocking voice contradicts me. He makes a rude noise with his fingers to his mouth.

"Yes," I say. "I need a company of brave knights to serve me."

"With horses and armor?" asks Toby.

"And swords," adds Jacob. They are both eager for position.

"I cannot give you any of those things yet," I say. "For now all you really need is a warrior's courage."

Mark stands and says—rather too loudly—"We be farmers' sons. There be dirt and toil in our future, not armor, horses, and swords."

I stood close to the bars and said in a strong, confident voice, "I can make knights of anyone I choose." It is true. A king or queen can do exactly that. "I do not care whose sons they are, as long as they have stout hearts."

Enid reaches up and pulls Mark down again and he squats on his heels quietly.

Jacob cries out, "My heart be stout. Once I saw off a mad dog with but a broken branch and a few stones. Ask anybody in Lanercost."

"It be true," Toby agrees. "I seen it."

"Make me a knight!" Jacob demands. Then he adds in a milder voice, "If it pleases ye."

"Come closer then," I say. I know that a king uses a sword to knight people, but I have nothing like that. Then I have a thought. I pull up the cord and hold Uncle Neil's ring in my hand.

Reaching my arm through the bars, I tap each of the brothers on the shoulder with the ring.

"With this ring that lately belonged to one of the kingdom's greatest, courageous, and most courteous of knights, I dub thee Sir Toby and Sir Jacob," My voice trembles a little. "To be knights in secret until the day I can openly declare it."

The two boys do not notice the tremor in my voice. They rise and proudly pound each other on the back, making much more noise than Mark ever did.

"Shut yer yaps, ye fools," Mark hisses at them.

They shut up at once and crouch down again, but they are grinning.

"See," Enid says happily, "it be just like Ma says. We be princes and princesses one day and live in castles and ride horses and things."

"She's talking about Heaven, ye nit," Mark says with a sneer, "where we will all be soon enow if we be found here."

Enid looks down, clearly hurt. It is clear she wants Mark to think well of her.

"No," I say. "Your mother is not speaking of Heaven. Have you not listened to the priests? Anything that is possible in Heaven is possible here and now. Like loving, and forgiving your enemies."

"Like being royal," Enid adds eagerly.

Mark makes another rude sound, this time through his nose. Like a horse.

"Lady Enid is right," I say, admonishing him in front of the others, but sweetly. "What is inside a person makes one royal. Not birth. Nor lands. Christ said as much."

It is the first argument that seems to sway Mark, and he grunts a kind of approval.

Enid seems to relax.

"And like Christ, the king should be both master and servant. And sometimes suffer for his people's sake." The girls nod at this but the boys do not seem to take it in. So I add, "As knights do, in battle, or in captivity." And at this they nod as well.

"Will you let me make you a knight then?" I say to Mark.

I do not get to hear his answer, because just then there is a noise at the gate and the children scramble away, doing their best to bow before they depart. They are suddenly mere shadows in the shadows.

The guards reappear, then pass on. Clearly they have seen nothing.

And I am alone again.

But no longer quite so lonely.

I have added knights to my realm.

Holding Uncle Neil's ring up so that it catches a bit of the moonlight, I press it to my lips. If the boys of Lanercost can be half as brave as he, they will make me fine knights indeed.

Early in the morning, before anyone else is awake, I manage to read six pages of my book, hunched over as if I had a belly ache. I am afraid that St. Cuthbert's life is not very compelling. But it is all that I have.

However, most of the day I hide the book away, under my skirts. That makes pacing and sitting a bit tricky. But anywhere else in this open cage, it would be seen.

In the evening I hide in the privy and hold the book up above the curtain, toward the waning moon. There is only enough light for me to get through a single page before my eyes begin to water. It does not matter. The page recounts Cuthbert's years as a shepherd. The author tells more about the sheep than the shepherd.

A noise outside prompts me to stick the book beneath the privy pot, and I lift the curtain to peek outside.

It is Enid and Ruth. They are creeping through the darkness like a pair of poachers. I am delighted to see them, but am downcast that none of the boys—my knights—is present.

"Apologies, yer queenship, but Mark canna come," Enid says immediately. "He be watching our old ewe all night cos she be ready to throw a harvest lamb. He must run and wake Da when she be bloody."

Ruth puts in, "Toby and Jacob tried to sneak away but their Ma caught them."

"She sent them back to bed with a slap round the ears," Enid adds.

"They be coming on the morrow." Ruth is eager to please me. "They be loyal knights, miss." She curtsies.

"Ma'am," Enid corrects.

"Remind them not to get too close or say anything out of turn," I warn.

They both nod.

"I be bringing ye this," says Ruth, passing an object through the bars.

It is a comb, crudely carved from a piece of dark wood. At first I can only think how primitive it is compared to the combs I am used to. Then I realize how precious such a thing must be to her. And how much I can use it.

"Surely this is your own," I say, offering it back to her. "I can not possibly take it."

"Oh, yer highness, keep it," Ruth insists. "When will there ever be a time when I'll have sommat a princess is without?"

She is right, of course, and to refuse the gift further would be an insult.

"Thank you," I say, and put the comb in my bodice, where it pricks like a dozen pins. "Alas—I have nothing to give you in return."

They inch closer to the cage and put their hands on the bars.

"Just tell us things," says Ruth.

"What things?"

"Things about . . . being a princess," they say together. There is such hunger in their voices, I begin at once.

I tell them about Lochmaben and my embroideries.

"I never seen embroideries," Ruth says.

"Yes—in church," Enid reminds her.

"Well, I sit on embroidered chairs," I say. "And there are hangings on the wall, a rug from Flanders."

Even though they do not know where Flanders is, they are impressed.

Next I talk about Kildrummy, that eagle's nest, and about the banquet in the Great Hall. I tell them about the slices of venison and boar that were served.

"We canna have such," Enid says. "Though the monks can."

Ruth nods.

"Why not?" I ask.

"That food be not for such as us," Enid says. "A man can be hanged for taking the earl's deer."

I had not known that. But I do not want to talk of hangings. If we talk of hangings, I shall remember other kinds of death. So I tell them about the Snow Tower. When I speak of the tapestries decorating the walls—the scenes of huntsmen carrying a dead wolf, the deer floundering in steep drifts, the angels descending on swanlike wings—they clap their hands. I have to shush them.

"It sounds a magical sort of place." Enid's voice is breathless, awed.

"Yes, it is," I say, remembering. Not only magic. Kildrummy was the last safe haven I knew.

And as quickly I remember why it is safe no more.

But this last I do not tell them.

In the morning, waking early once more, I manage three more pages of Cuthbert and his sheep while sitting in the privy. I have just gotten to the place where he enters a monastery, which is more promising than the sheep. I have hope for some miracles now.

Suddenly I hear a noise beyond the curtains.

I tuck the book beneath the piss pot, and crawl out.

It is my royal chaplain, but this day he does not stay with me. Instead he delivers my breakfast—more glutinous porridge—then scurries off as fast as his ill-fitting robe will let him.

Poor man. He runs like a goose.

But I can hardly blame him. He has both Longshanks and his own abbot to fear. The abbot can put him on bread and water, I suppose, and make him kneel for hours on the hard stone floors in penance.

I do not like to think what Longshanks might do.

The thought makes my eyes prick with tears. I clutch Uncle Neil's ring so hard in my hand, the thistle leaves an imprint on my palm.

I pass another boring morning, gazing at the priory, counting birds that fly overhead. The day is crisp and cooling. I worry that it will soon be cold. I wonder if I dare ask Enid and Ruth to get me a bit of wool to wrap under my skirt. No one will see it if I am careful. I can cover myself at night after Longshanks has been to visit.

At the morning's hind end, a small group of seven boys comes ambling up the road. They are not local boys, for I recognize none of them. From their clothes, they are not peasants' sons. They wear well-made tunics and clean hose darned with careful stitchery. One boy even has a cape. Perhaps their fathers are blacksmiths or carpenters or wheelwrights. Men of more substance than Enid and Ruth's fathers. Perhaps they are students at the priory, though I have not seen them before.

I sit on the floor of the cage and examine them without appearing to look their way.

There is some pointing and sniggering, things I am well used to by this time. And some new words that are clearly swears, which I have not heard before.

"She's too snooty a cow for the likes of us," one of the boys calls out.

"Well, she shouldna be," says another. "Filthy thing. Look at her!"

And a third, "Why's her nose in the air? She's the one locked up in a kennel."

"Pigsty, more like," says the first.

This brings a peal of laughter from them and a flush to my face. I turn away slightly.

But they are right, of course. I have not had water to bathe in for a fortnight. Ruth's comb has made only slight inroads into the tangles of my hair. I have not been allowed to change out of this dress the entire time of my imprisonment. It is grey with fatigue, with wear, with filth. The pigs back at Lochmaben were surely better kept than I.

There are more insults and more jokes.

"Phew, what stink!" That was the boy in the cape.

"Oink . . . oink . . . oink!" cried another.

Someone makes a noise like a fart.

I wonder where my guards are now. Still, I am careful not to look at the boys. I yawn.

And then the missiles come, rotted vegetables, some balls of manure. I barely have to move to dodge them. Honestly, they are so predictable! Even the people of Lanercost have given up such sport.

Then one of the boys sneaks around the other side of the cage, from the back, and I do not notice him. He flings a rock about the size of a baby's fist. It misses the bars and strikes me directly on the cheek. The shock of it, and the stinging pain, knocks me forward onto my stomach.

The boys break out into a chorus of cheers.

"Good shot, Will!" one of them calls. "Watch this one!"

Another rock strikes me in the back and this time I cannot keep the tears from my eyes.

Suddenly I hear fresh voices. I think: This time I may be killed.

Dear Lord, I pray, do not let me die in a cage. I want to live. No, even more, I want to outlive my tormentors. I want to give Father a hug and Elizabeth a kiss once more. I want to sing with Maggie again. I want to be brave.

That is when I realize the shouts are not for my blood.

"Clear off, ye bastards! Ye've no business here!"

Someone is coming to my rescue.

Cautiously I sit up and through watery eyes I see Toby and Jacob galloping toward the newcomers, Mark at their heels.

"Clear off, should we?" one of the stone throwers sneers. "Ain't we a right to our share of fun?"

Another adds, "Ye Lanercoster farm boys canna keep sech sport to yer own selves."

Toby plants himself between my cage and the other boys. "She's a princess," he tells them. "We be her knights."

Jacob takes up a position at his side.

"Knights!" laugh the newcomers. They are very brave as Toby and Jacob are smaller than they. "Nits more like it!"

Their leader adds, "And what kind of princess? She's naught but a puir mad girl in a cage."

Jacob squares his shoulders. "And what kind o' creatures do ye be, throwing rocks at a 'puir mad girl in a cage'?"

The boy in the cape has an answer for that. "We've rocks enow for ye toads as well."

Without warning, Mark—who is as big as the caped boy—steps forward and lays him flat with one blow of his fist.

The fallen boy howls with pain, sounding like a stuck pig.

"Don't just stand there," he squeals at his companions. "Get them!"

The two sides fall upon each other in a flurry of punches, kicks, and scratches.

My hands clutch the bars of the cage till the knuckles turn white. Dear Lord, I pray, protect my knights.

Mark and his two cousins strike out as boldly as any warriors, but slowly they are beaten back. Seven to three is not a fair fight.

Then two guards, alerted by the noise, come running down from the priory. They are carrying spears.

Thank you, Lord, I whisper as they push the two sides apart with the butt ends of their weapons.

"Off!" they tell the boys. "Away! Or there will be more than banged heads."

The attackers take to their heels and Mark leads a cheer for our side, shouting, "Run, run ye yellow-livered bumpkins."

One of the guards silences him with a jab in the midriff. "This girl's a traitor to the king and is to be treated as such."

Mark glares at him, but the guard gives him another shove. "Now get off home before I lock ye up as traitors, too."

My noble little band retreats toward the village. But they carry themselves with pride.

Toby dares a look over his shoulder at me and I wave at him. I hope he understands how grateful I am.

The guard who had poked Mark sticks his spear butt into the cage and shoves me back. "Stir up any more trouble, girl, and it will go hard with ye."

"It is already going hard with me," I say as he turns away. I am not afraid of him, I, who can hold my own with his miserable, dying king.

But, I think, perhaps things will go a little less hard now, for I do not just have royal knights.

I have an army.

I spend the afternoon thinking about how fiercely the boys fought for me. I chuckle remembering each blow, each fierce cry.

But then, just as I am enjoying myself, Longshanks pays me another visit.

I suddenly remember that I left the book in its hiding place under the piss pot. I have not put it back beneath my skirts. The comb in my bosom begins to prick me. Have I let a small victory make me careless? What kind of a general would I make?

I am not afraid for myself. It is my chaplain for whom I am afraid. He could be sorely punished for my carelessness. So I try my best to look calm and unconcerned as the litter is set down only a few feet from the bars.

There is this peculiar thing about guilt. The more you try to look innocent, the more you look guilty. My cheeks flame. I fear that if I open my mouth, I will stutter like the monk. I put a hand up to my hair. It is still tangled but not as bad as before. Will Longshanks notice? Will he guess what that means?

Dear Lord, help me. And as I pray, my cheeks grow cool again.

Longshanks signals for the litter bearers to leave him, but he seems too ill today to stand. For such a tall man he seems strangely shrunken.

He stares up at me from beneath heavy eyelids, his face so chalky, he almost looks like a statue on the lid of a tomb. His nose is a beak today, his lips bloodless, thinned down to a slash.

"I hear you have instigated some of the peasant children to violence on your behalf," he says in a dull voice.

This is no time for silence. I must defend my defenders. "They were just playing," I said. "I am certain they meant no harm." I drew in a careful breath. "It was the other boys, the outsiders, who began it."

His thin lips curve into a slow smile, the old serpent again. "Did they? I wonder."

"Yes," I say, warming to the story, "the other boys came and threw rocks so—"

He interrupts me with a question that takes my breath away. "How many times have the Lanercost boys been visiting you by night?"

Before I can deny it, my face has given its own flaming answer.

"It would have to be by night when the clods who are supposed to be standing guard are dozing on their feet," he says.

I am taken aback by how easily he is able to deduce the truth. For all his illness, his mind is still frighteningly sharp.

But I must be sharp, too. "No one comes close unless it is to torment me," I say. "You know that only too well. No one except the monk who feeds me."

Almost as if summoned by my words, the monk appears with my supper. He performs his duties nervously under Longshanks' watchful eye, sliding cup and bowl and spoon to me, then making himself scarce.

The king watches him go with glittering eyes. Then he waves his brightly garbed attendant closer.

"Double the guards this side of the priory," he instructs in a rasping voice. "And see they make regular sweeps of the area through the night. I do not want anyone to torment my prize." He smiles my way. "Except me."

With that he signals to his men and they lift the litter up again, leaving me alone once more.

My royal chaplain appears more nervous than ever when he brings my breakfast. He looks over his shoulder as if the devil were behind him. I think that if he could have delivered the bowl and its watery contents without coming anywhere near me, he would have leapt at the chance. As it is he, he sets bowl and spoon and cup down and goes back to the priory at once.

I try to make the thin porridge last, but it is gone too soon. So I hide in the privy and read three more pages of Cuthbert, who is now happily in his monastery.

In the middle of a sentence, I hear sounds outside. Shoving the book into my linens, I walk out to the main part of the cage, adjusting my skirts as if I had just relieved myself.

There is Longshanks in his litter. Though it is morning, he is heading this way.

Four soldiers accompany him. Each one carries a large, heavy wooden bucket. They take up positions on all four sides of the cage.

"What is going on?" I cry.

"Your cage has become unacceptably filthy," he answers, "and so have you. I trust we can wash your dirt away and your insolence with it."

He twitches an upraised finger by way of a signal and the first of the nearest of the soldiers heaves his bucket in my direction, sloshing cold water all across the floor of the cage.

I jump to keep the water from slopping over my boots, but a second bucketful comes from behind me. I want a bath, but not like this.

The water splashes over my back and down to the floor and I gasp as a shiver shakes my entire body.

"Stop!" I cry. I do not mean to make a sound, but it comes out anyway. Though the day is warm enough for October, the water is fresh from the river. It feels like ice.

A faint smile plays about Longshanks' pale lips. He is enjoying this. It is more than just a punishment.

"What do you want of me?" I ask, my arms clutched over the front of my dress.

"Only that which I demand of all my subjects," Longshanks replies. His voice is brittle with anger. "Your submission to my will."

"But I am *not* one of your subjects," I say, struggling to keep my teeth from chattering.

"Of course you are," he retorts angrily. "Do you not realize that it is only a pitiful remnant of your countrymen who continue to defy me? What chance have you here, girl, directly under my hand?"

"Even a few will be enough," I say, "if they are true Scots."

He laughs. "I am the Hammer of the Scots," he says. "And all who defy me will be shattered on the anvil of their own devising."

"Then go do your work," I tell him, too cold now to care.

Longshanks makes an impatient noise at the back of his

throat and nods to his soldiers. Both remaining buckets are flung together, one at my waist and one striking me in the face, like a cold, wet fist.

I stumble backward, brush against the curtained privy and slam into the iron bars.

Something slips down between my legs as if I am giving birth. It lands on the floor of the cage with a thud.

"What is that?" Longshanks exclaims. He climbs from the litter and comes over the cage to see for himself.

I shrug, as if I do not know, but of course I do. Poor Cuthbert. I am already cold and miserable and wet. Now I turn into ice.

Longshanks stares goggle-eyed at the slim volume as though it were a bloody dagger. One of his attendants runs forward. He stretches an arm into the cage, snatching up the book and delivering it to his master, who grips the cover so tightly, his veins stand out like thick blue cords on the back of his hand. Then he flips through the pages before snapping it shut.

"Who gave you this?" he demands through gritted teeth.

I turn my ice head away and refuse to answer. I will not betray a member of my court.

"It makes no difference what you say," he tells me. "The guilty party is all too obvious."

I turn and glare at him, raising one eyebrow. I have seen Father do this. Usually at Uncle Neil.

He continues. "No peasant child has brought you this. They cannot read, so why should any of them own such a precious object as a book?" He turns through the damp pages slowly, as if searching for an answer. Then suddenly he looks up and snaps his fingers. "Who was that monk who, yesterday, brought you food?"

I cannot answer. I do not know the man's name.

"I believe he is called Quintus," says one of the guards.

I have to make some effort to protect Brother Quintus, no matter how futile it might be.

"There are any number of ways I could have come by that book," I say. "You are foolish to guess."

Longshanks ignores me. "Bring me this Quintus," he says.

"That book is the life of a saint," I say. I keep my voice even. I must not beg. "Surely only good comes from reading such a thing. Is not every prisoner entitled to the comfort of God's word?"

Longshanks scowls. "You are not every prisoner and I did not sanction it." Holding the book in both hands, he rips it clean down the middle and scatters the pages across the grass like dead leaves.

I am appalled. I wonder suddenly if Cuthbert is watching from his place in Heaven.

Longshanks' face is flushed from the exertion. For the first time he willingly leans on his attendants' shoulders. He allows himself to be nudged, lifted, poured back into the litter where he waves a weary hand to the bearers, who start toward the priory.

I gaze at the precious pages Longshanks has destroyed. The autumn breeze plucks at them and flips them over as though toying with the plucked feathers of a dead bird.

The October sun for once is strong and there is no cooling breeze. The sun bakes out my wet clothes and dries my hair.

Now that I am dry again—if not exactly warm—I can even thank Longshanks for my bath. I do not think I stink as badly as before. I would comb out my hair with Ruth's comb if I could do it without being seen. But I would not like to get her in trouble, too. I must wait to do that in the dark.

Supper is brought by a different monk this time, an angular man with hooded eyes and the long lean face of a hungry goat.

"What has happened to . . . to Brother Quintus?" I ask.

He is silent; his hooded eyes do not even flicker. He passes bowl and cup and spoon through the bars.

"Is he all right?"

The new monk is silent as stone. I might as well be talking to the statue of a saint. His duty done, he departs.

I resist *maa*ing like a goat to his back. But just.

Picking at my meager meal, I wonder if I have made things worse by asking about Brother Quintus by name. My appetite has abandoned me. This is strange. Normally I am starving. But I can not eat for worrying about the round-faced monk with the graying tonsure who ran like a goose and who sat with me on the day I wept for Uncle Neil. So little has passed between us, yet I think of him as a friend. I fear what his king has in mind.

Later, when hunger gnaws at me, I finish the gruel, then sit cross-legged, trying to remember the details of St. Cuthbert's story. There is a lull in the evening, as if everyone in Lanercost is sleeping off a heavy meal.

A hawk with sharp wings swoops onto a tree near the priory gate and stares at me. No one else is around. Even the guards are gone. After a minute the hawk flaps away. There is no meal for it here.

What does this mean? Am I allowed to hope that Longshanks has forgotten or forgiven the faults of my court? Is it too much to hope?

I almost start a small prayer of gratitude when suddenly, a group of eight soldiers marches purposefully up the road from the village where they have been quartered. They stomp their way noisily into the priory.

I fear it has begun, though I do not know what "it" is.

I stand and come close to the bars of the cage, not wanting to miss a moment.

Four of the soldiers come back out quickly through the priory gate, rolling a hay wagon that has but two large wheels. They park it about twenty yards from my cage and then stand at attention.

A second group of eight soldiers comes up from the village leading a crowd of peasants. I glimpse Enid and Ruth and the three boys in their midst but I make no sign to them.

Be silent, I will them. Whatever is happening, do not say a word!

There is another flurry of movement through the gates and all the monks, now in white robes, file out and form up near the wall. At their head is a man who, by his bearing, is clearly the abbot. He has a high, intelligent forehead and bright, keen eyes. I do not think he likes what he sees.

But what is it he sees? I cannot guess. No—I do not want to guess.

The soldiers sort themselves into ranks and at last Longshanks appears in his litter. He seems satisfied at this orderly little kingdom. But should he ask me, I would tell him that order drawn up out of fear is no order at all.

And there is fear here. I can smell it. It smells like iron on a smith's anvil, hot and bitter.

Lord, I pray, do not let anything happen to me now.

Or, I add quickly, Brother Quintus.

I scan the faces of the monks, but there is one I do not see. Only now do I guess the worst. I clutch Uncle Neil's ring in my left hand. My right hand is around one of the bars.

"No," I whisper to myself. "Please, no."

Just then Brother Quintus is brought out through the gate under an armed escort. The soldiers push him forward so roughly, his feet become tangled in his robe. He falls to his knees.

Laughter ripples through the crowd. I think it comes more from the soldiers than the folk of Lanercost. After all, Longshanks and his army are strangers, but the monks have lived here forever.

Clambering painfully to his feet, my poor chaplain looks for help in the direction of his abbot.

The abbot's face is without expression. I had a governess like that once. Nothing I did ever pleased her.

Poor Brother Quintus. He is pushed down on what must be sore knees. When he looks up, his face is puzzled, frightened. He is not a soldier after all.

And even a soldier would be afraid.

At last Longshanks speaks. "It was your duty, monk, to fetch the prisoner's meals and tend to her privy, nothing more. You were specifically told to hold no converse with her and give her no succor. But you did not listen." Longshanks waves in the direction of the torn fragments of the book still fluttering in the grass. "You gave her a book in defiance of my stated commands."

Brother Quintus glances helplessly from Longshanks to his abbot and back again. He finds no help there. Then he makes a fatal mistake—he looks at me.

Longshanks reaches over and grabs Brother Quintus' nose, pulling him forward. "Deny it if you will and blacken your soul with one more sin."

"M-my lord, I b-beg you," Brother Quintus stammers, reaching for his nose, yet afraid to touch the royal hand.

"Beg mercy of God," Longshanks says. "You will get none from me." He lets go and Brother Quintus rocks back. But there is no escape. Longshanks gives a curt signal with his hand to the captain of his guard.

Two soldiers haul Brother Quintus to his feet and drag him to the wagon. They bend him forward over the wheel and tie his wrists to the spokes with strips of leather.

I cannot watch. I cannot.

I start to close my eyes.

But then I think—I was not there to commit Uncle Neil's death to memory. I did not see Seton die. I am a princess of Scotland and I must be a witness for my own.

I will myself to be strong and open my eyes.

The soldiers rip Brother Quintus' robe to his waist, exposing his soft, pale back. Another soldier approaches carrying a lash made of several lengths of knotted cord.

Not an execution then, I think, letting go of the breath I am holding, though I had not known it was being held. Still, I have heard that a badly beaten man can die of his wounds.

Shaking, I cry out to Longshanks, "Punish me, not him. A gentle heart is his only crime."

"*Treason* is his only crime," says Longshanks. "So, by rights I could take his life, except his life is the abbot's property."

At that the abbot shuffles from one foot to the other, but he does not try to intervene. I guess that the abbot is the one who gave this argument to Longshanks. But behind closed doors.

He cannot be happy seeing one of his monks so badly used. They are supposed to be brothers, after all.

I know about brothers. My father has four.

Had.

He *had* four.

I think of Uncle Neil and harden my heart.

"Commence!" Longshanks barks.

The soldier with the whip raises it high and brings it down with a crack. The first stroke brings red weals to Brother Quintus' back and tears to my eyes. I feel the stroke myself as if it is my own back.

Again and again the lash is laid across his unprotected flesh, white like the flesh of a sheep that has been badly shorn. Soon his poor back is streaked with blood.

I know that Brother Quintus is only an ordinary man. Not a hero. Not a saint. Not a martyr. But what an awful price to pay for a simple act of kindness.

At the first few blows he merely whimpers. Then, as the wounds cut deeper, he cries out in agony.

The whine of the lash and Brother Quintus' sobs are the only sounds to be heard. The soldiers, the other monks, the villagers—even Longshanks and his peacock of an attendant—all look on in silence.

I flinch with every blow but I watch. I am stony-eyed. I am steel.

I think about how my father must feel each time he learns of his followers being tortured and executed. It is a high price for being king. How does he bear it? I cannot.

After twenty-five lashes, the soldiers untie Brother Quintus and let him slump to the ground.

I slump, too, still holding on to the bars.

Overhead a pair of gulls quarrel noisily. No one looks up. We are all watching Brother Quintus.

The abbot sends two brothers to attend him. They raise him up gently. He winces when they touch his arms. There are dark tear tracks down his cheeks. He leans against them heavily as they take him inside.

At a command from their captain, the soldiers send the villagers back to the village and usher the remaining monks into the priory. Only Longshanks, his attendant, the litter bearers and the captain of the guard remain outside.

"And *now* you will accept me as your liege lord," Longshanks rasps as he climbs from his litter and all alone comes over to my cage. "Just as all these others do."

Suddenly I feel cold. And old. I have left childhood far behind.

He waits with a hand wrapped around the cage bars. Waiting for my response.

I glare at him. "You call *that* acceptance?" My voice is deep, low. I think I sound like Elizabeth now. "They only accept you out of fear, not out of love."

Longshanks laughs. "Love is a poor foundation for a throne."

"Tell that to the people who love my father and who are willing to give their lives for him."

Longshanks is suddenly seized by a fit of coughing. His usually yellow face turns near purple. There are veins at his temple that seem ready to burst. With a colossal effort he regains control of himself.

"And do *you* so love your father?" he asks. His face in repose becomes snakelike. His eyes are slits.

I know what he is asking. It is the ultimate test. The final battle.

"Of course," I say.

"If you want to die for your father, then you shall have your wish!" he says. He turns to the captain of the guards. "Stop her meals. Have guards set a twenty-foot perimeter around the cage to ensure no one comes near her. Kill anyone who tries to bring her food or drink." He staggers back to his litter, climbs in, and lies there alternately coughing and gasping for breath.

As I watch, he is carried to his apartments within the priory and he does not once look back.

31 ❧ THE SIXTEENTH DAY OF MY CAPTIVITY

The sky has been clouding over all afternoon and now there is a sudden, welcome shower. If this had been a cold March downpour or a frigid December rain I might not be so pleased with it. But I am happy to note that Longshanks has no control over the winds and rains.

I have been a day without food, a day since Longshanks stopped the little bit I was allowed. Already my empty belly is complaining. All morning it growled, but now it actually aches.

I stretch my arms through the bars and cup my hands to catch some drops of precious water. I can only bring a little in at a time. So I hold my skirt out in the rain until it is well soaked, then I sit down and suck on the skirt like a teat.

The water is sweeter than any I have ever tasted. But the little bit I get only teases my stomach. The ache grows stronger. Suddenly I wonder if I have made a mistake. Perhaps I should not try to slow my dying.

My dying! It is only one day and already I am dwelling on the end.

But then I think: Each day I live is a day that Longshanks must watch me die.

I hold out the skirt in the rain once more. Every small mouthful feels like a triumph over him.

From the cage I can see eight soldiers in their green surcoats and shiny helmets. They are stationed at various points, each an equal distance from my cage. It is as if invisible lines run from guard to guard, and these lines form the outer wall of my prison. Invisible bars around an invisible cage.

They have been standing at attention that way all day. Last night they lit lanterns and patrolled the area in crisscrossing patterns. Making certain, I suppose, that no one tries to reach me under cover of darkness.

And, of course, no one tries.

Now the rain is easing. I do not know if it will come again. I have sucked out all the moisture from my dress and long for more. I look up into the darkening sky and feel like a farmer desperate for rain.

A pair of monks pass by, silent as ever. Their heads are bent, their eyes on the path at their feet. They are careful not to step over the invisible lines.

I call out, "Pray for me, brothers."

But they do not look up.

My belly growls. I push my fist into it to try and quiet the complaint.

I think about all those days when I was fleeing with my aunts and Elizabeth and Isabel through the Highlands. How I existed on nettle soup and water from the swift rushing streams.

I think of the two long weeks I have been in this cage. Eating thin gruel and rotting vegetables.

See—I tell myself—you are already accustomed to starvation. What is a bit less?

I will not complain aloud. I will not give my captors satisfaction. And if Longshanks comes by to gloat, he will be disappointed. He will find me unrepentant and unbowed.

Three more days now without food. It is impossible to ignore the stab of hunger in my belly. It is all I can think about: this throbbing ache that will not go away. That and food.

I think about food all the time. Slabs of venison, pink and bloody. A large serving of boar surrounded by pears and chestnuts. A board of hot bread straight from the oven. Milk fresh from the cow. Butter fresh from the churn.

I have not had anything to drink since the rain. I do not even pass water anymore.

Last night I woke moaning and calling for Maggie to bring me something to ease the pain. It was a struggle to get back to sleep.

This morning brings no relief. Hour by sorry hour the day drags by while the pain grows like a hungry beast eating me up from the inside.

Though the day is grey and cold, I am warm. I feel light-headed and heavy-headed at the same time. My brow is feverish. My skin feels stretched over hollow bones. I must lie down. Standing up is too hard.

Dear Lord, dying is more difficult than I had supposed.

Through all of the day, the soldiers never glance at me. It is as if this cage were empty. As if it is the air inside that they are guarding.

I cannot blame the guards. They are only obeying orders. They will guard me the same if I am alive or dead.

Would I know if I were dead? Are there not dead who walk denying their deaths?

I turn over on my back and gaze through the bars at the cold sky. White feathers are falling, as if angels descend from Heaven, coming to carry me away.

I try to hold up my arms. But my arms are too heavy. Then I blink twice, and turn over on my belly. Surely angels would be flying toward me, not walking along the village road.

I blink a second time. This time I see that the drifting feathers are really snowflakes. How strange, I think, for I am not cold at all.

At the third blink I see that the angels are village children—Enid and Ruth and Toby and Jacob and others.

Mark is in the midst of them, his face a mask of determination.

"Back!" orders a soldier. "Get back to yer work and yer homes!"

"We be from Lanercost," Enid declares boldly, "and we can stay on the road if we like."

"Not if the king says ye can't," says another of the soldiers. They close in on the children. "Now clear off!"

I try to wave them away, my brave little court. I do not want them beaten. But again my arms are too heavy. I can only move my fingers a tiny bit, a motion no one sees.

The soldiers shove the children, their hands on Enid and Ruth particularly, for those two are leading the little band. Toby ducks under the soldiers' arms, making faces and letting out rude noises. Two boys follow him.

In the midst of this distraction, Mark dodges to one side and flings a missile toward the cage.

It turns end over end as it arcs through the air in a strange, slow way. The snowflakes seem to part before it. How odd, I think as I watch it fall. When it lands short of the cage and bounces on the dried grass, I see it is a bread roll.

A bread roll!

A flake of snow settles upon it like a sprinkling of sweet icing.

My stomach clenches. What I would give for a bite.

The captain has spotted this attempt to feed me and in one stride he is looming over Mark. Before my brave knight can make a move to protect himself, he is punched in the stomach and folds up on the ground like an empty sack.

The other children yell and squeal in protest. Three boys try to jump on one soldier's back and are beaten off.

"Da, help!" Ruth cries out over and over. "Help us!"

Some men come running up from the village.

And all the while the snow keeps falling, white and pure.

One of the village men takes up a stand over Mark, meeting the captain's stare with a ferocious glower of his own. He must be Mark's father. He has the same round head, thin reddish hair, though his hairline starts farther back. His fingers twitch angrily on the mattock he holds in his hand. The snow swirls around his head like a halo.

"We thought ye be here to defend us, not make war on our children." He speaks like a bear, all grunts and growls.

"Ye know the king's command," says the captain. "It binds both young and old."

While they talk I inch my way across the floor of the cage till

I am pressed up against the bars. Slowly I push my hand through. The air outside the cage feels thick and unyielding. I reach for the bread roll through the falling snow.

Alas—the roll is much too far away. But I believe my arm will grow longer just by willing it. I think: grow, for Jesus' sake, grow!

The captain walks over to the roll and his leather boot stomps downward, grinding it into crumbs. He speaks not a word to me. The villagers watch in simmering silence.

Then the guards return to their stations, the villagers to their homes, and I am left here in the cage, watching as sparrows hop through the falling snow and gobble up the crumbs.

Time slips by like sand emptying from an hourglass and—at long last—he is here.

Longshanks.

My old enemy.

The snow suddenly stops. I wonder—can a king command the snow?

The sky is the color of weathered stone.

I can see Longshanks walking toward me, his litter some distance behind. His men are cautious, keeping well back from the cage.

Should I stand?

Can I stand?

I wonder that I am so heavy who is now so light. Yet I manage to sit up slowly, with the help of angels at each arm. I take hold of the bars, pulling myself to my feet.

It is like hauling up a sack full of stones.

I run my tongue over my lips, but they are both so dry, I am afraid they will stick together.

My legs are as feeble as straw. I have to lean against the bars to remain upright. But at least I am not bowing before the wrong king.

Longshanks' face is yellow, his eyes tinged with a feverish crimson. His mouth curls into an empty smile that clearly costs him much effort.

"Nature tries to drag me down, but I have fought back," he says in a voice so thin, only I can hear it. "I have taken an elixir in which gold, silver, and pearls have been steeped. They will lend me their healthy luster."

He drinks jewels while others eat dirt. I hope he chokes on his own wealth. I try to tell him this but my throat closes down.

He is still talking. I have trouble following what he says. Something about more castles and towns. Something about everything falling before his armies. Something about how happy the Scots are under his rule.

I look up at the grey weathered sky. Is it stone? I think it is stone. Soon it will fall down. Down it will come, on my head, on Longshanks. We will both be dead then, but Father will have won.

I look away from the sky and watch Longshanks' thin lips. They are still flapping.

"*Blah-blah, blah,*" he says.

I strain harder to listen.

"And yet you, a prisoner here," he says, "*blah-blah-di-blah.*"

It still makes no sense.

"Resist me to your own sorry ruination," he says.

I do not understand what he means. I remember only that Father will win.

"Father." I whisper that one word. It is not what he wants to hear.

"Your *father.*" He spits the word out in drool. "You cling to your father as a sinner clings to his sin. But I will cure you of that." He leans his head into the cage, the bars catching him at the temples. "Renounce him, girl, and accept me as your king."

"Why?" I rasp. I mean why should I do something dying that I would not do when well.

He misunderstands.

"Because then I will release you from this cage. I will see that you are housed in one of my royal manors, with new clothes and servants and a soft bed covered with silken sheets."

I do not want that.

"Food," I say.

He grins. "Yes, of course, food. Platters filled with every manner of fish and fowl, fresh spring water and the sweetest wines."

For a moment I see the joints of meat, the loaves and pastries, the cups brimming with delicious water. It all dances before my eyes.

Then I remember Christ in the desert and all the temptations he refused, and blink them away.

Blearily I gaze at Longshanks' face, a wrinkled map of bitterness and pain.

Is he telling me the truth?

I think he is. I think he would pay almost any price for my surrender.

But he has misjudged me.

He has misjudged the Scots.

With an effort I close my eyes and shake my head.

"You are destroying yourself to no purpose!" Longshanks is almost choking on his frustration. "The weak must give way to the strong. That is the way of things."

Slowly I open my eyes. I will make an effort. "And . . . if the . . . weak . . . will not . . . give way?" I whisper.

"They must, as surely as the trees bow before the blast of winter." He clenches his fist and beats it against the bars of the cage. "They must! How could it be otherwise?"

I am seized by dizziness. My legs buckle beneath me. I want to force myself to stand because his words are like a riddle that I must solve. I am certain that if I can give him the answer I will have won.

But I cannot. And I can no longer stand. I crumple to the floor of the cage, my fingers sliding down the cold length of the iron bars. Darkness and my own exhaustion overwhelm me.

33 ❧ THE TWENTIETH DAY OF MY CAPTIVITY

Mother!"

I am startled awake by the sound of my own voice calling out. I was dreaming of home and a face appeared before me. Not Isabel of Mar, the dead mother I had never known, but Elizabeth, who had been ready to give her life for mine.

This, I am certain, is the final day of my life. Of course it is difficult to think clearly when you have not eaten for days. The fire in your belly blots out everything else. The harsh glare of the sun can blind you if you look too long at it.

I pass my time in a strange state halfway between waking and sleeping. It is difficult to be sure now what I am really seeing and what is merely a dream.

I think I can see playmates from my childhood days skipping through the fields: the son of the steward, the daughter of the cook.

There is Maggie in her dark dress with the white collar, and my aunts whispering and laughing, holding up their skirts and running across the lea.

Here comes Uncle Neil on Grey Glennie, his armor shining like pure silver in the sun. As he passes he draws his sword and salutes me, but I cannot see his face for the visor of his helmet. I would like to know if he is smiling, if he approves.

John of Atholl rides after him, his white beard clean and combed. And bold Christopher Seton waving his hand. And after them comes a whole host of dead warriors carrying Scotland's banner, the white cross on the blue field.

I know this is a delusion, and yet it seems so real. I blink and they disappear.

My real fear is that I have become mad, and that I will end up doing and saying whatever Longshanks wishes.

But perhaps he will not return. Perhaps he does not want to watch me die.

Or perhaps this is some sort of race to see which of us will die first: I, of neglect, or he, surrounded by doctors, courtiers, and priests.

Noon. A shrunken sun wanders in a slatey sky. I lie on my back in the cage and try to write between the grey clouds. Words. A prayer.

Suddenly, Longshanks is here at the cage, looking frailer than ever.

Or is he really here? Perhaps this is only another vision conjured out of my wandering mind.

I flip over on my stomach, and stare. He does not disappear.

"You have only a little time left," he tells me.

"Neither of us has . . . much . . . time," I manage to croak. "I am just . . . dying a little . . . faster than you."

He leans against the cage and wipes a trembling hand across his sweaty brow. I pull myself over to where he waits.

I smell the sourness of his breath.

No delusion then.

"I do not fear death," he says. His voice is as feeble as mine.

"I am a godly man. I led a crusading army against the heathen. Your great-grandfather traveled to the Holy Land with me." He stops, takes a breath. "If you Scots will but give me . . . peace . . . I will never again raise arms . . . against Christian men." Another deep breath. "I will return . . . to the Holy Land. Spend my last breath . . . warring against the enemies of Christ."

His words are as heavy as stones. They tire him. And I can not carry them all in my brain.

"I fight for the good . . . of my people. For the honor of . . . my God," Longshanks insists. He repeats, "I am a godly king."

His body is shaken by a sudden spasm of coughing. When it subsides, he sinks to his knees. His cheek rests against the bars of my cage. Now we are almost nose to nose.

"Yield up, girl. There's no shame in it."

"I cannot." I manage to say, "I cannot . . . betray the dead."

"The dead?"

"Those you . . . have killed." Suddenly I have new strength and add in a rush, "I have seen them waiting to welcome me."

"Ghosts, you mean?" He looks about with wary eyes. "What do they want? Do they want . . . revenge?"

I shake my head, but slowly, carefully. My head is heavy. I am afraid it will break right off my neck. "No. They . . . pity you."

He tries to laugh but it comes out a hollow bark that shrivels to a rattling cough. The cough shakes him, like a terrier with a rat.

"Pity? Me? But they are dead. And I live," he says.

"Not for long," I tell him.

He stares at me and for the first time I do not see anger in his eyes. Or vanity. Or cruelty.

I see fear.

Suddenly I no longer feel my hunger, my frailty, my death. "That is why *I* pity you, too," I say. It is true. I am so close to dying, I can only speak the truth now.

He shakes his head, disbelieving.

"The people I see . . . died serving Scotland." I gather more strength. "But you will be dead . . . serving only yourself." I smile. My lips are so dry.

"Pah!" He rattles the bars with one hand. "You are raving. These are tales such as old women tell to frighten children."

Through cracked lips I whisper, "And who do you hope to be waiting for you . . . when you die?"

There is a long pause and he glances away, toward the sky. When he turns back, his voice is strangely hushed. "My wife Eleanor, dead these sixteen years. That is not too much to hope for." His eyes have a watery look, but it could simply be old age or the fact that the wind has picked up or that he has just been gazing into the sun. "I have married again, of course. A king must do that . . . for the kingdom. A young princess. From France. But it is not . . . not the same."

"You loved her then? Eleanor?" It is hard to believe this man ever loved anyone.

Again a pause, and a look away. As if he struggles to recall feelings long laid aside. "I built her . . . the most beautiful tomb in Christendom. At every point . . . where her funeral procession stopped . . . I raised a magnificent cross."

I am surprised at his passion. But then I think: Even a villain can feel passion for something.

"I am sure she waits for you," I say. I take a deep breath. "But first you will have to pass by all those you have killed." It comes out in a rush.

All at once Longshanks' watery eyes grow wide—and then hard. No longer water but stone. He turns and looks toward the priory. I turn my head to see what has worked this change.

For an instant I think that a band of ghosts has materialized out of the air before the priory walls. They are gauzy figures wreathed in shimmering grey. Then I realize that it is snowing again. What I am seeing are the monks in their long robes through a haze of snow.

Longshanks drags himself up until he is standing straight. His cheeks blaze with color. Anger fills him, lends him a last burst of strength.

Why is he so angry? I am not. I have given over my own anger. I am no longer happy or sad or frightened. I stare at the monks trying to make sense of Longshanks' mood.

The monks move forward, the abbot at their head. Their feet are invisible beneath their long robes and they seem to glide across the grass, like phantoms.

Then I see the most surprising thing of all. The abbot is holding a wooden tray on which is a small loaf of bread and a flask of water.

It takes me a moment before I understand that he is bringing this to me. I would hardly be more amazed if I beheld my father at the head of a great host come to break me free.

Longshanks grips the cage convulsively. I am certain he wants to go right up to the abbot and strike him down. But in his weakness, he dares not move for fear of falling. He coughs several times, then signals the captain, who has two of his spear men advance to block the monks.

At the same moment, there comes a hubbub from the village. Slowly I turn my head and see a great crowd hurrying up the grassy slope. They are men and women and children, all bustling and chattering, like a restless sea tide. Many of them carry axes, mattocks, scythes.

Some of the soldiers form up in a thin, nervous line before them.

It is a rebellion. And against their own lawful king.

Longshanks now casts baleful glances back and forth between the monks and the village folk. If he could stop them with a look, he would.

Then the abbot starts walking toward me once again. All eyes are upon him. He presses past the two guards, one of the spear points snagging briefly on the sleeve of his habit.

Longshanks pushes himself away from the cage, lurching into the abbot's path.

"What do you think you are doing?" he demands.

"Following God's acts of charity," says the abbot. "Feeding the hungry."

"As your king I command you to stop." Longshanks' arms flail as he forces himself to stand. Then anger takes over again and he draws himself up straight.

"Another king, higher than you, commands me to continue," says the abbot in a steady voice. "The brothers have sworn that we will carry out this duty, and you will have to kill each of us in turn before we will be stopped."

"This is treason!" Longshanks snarls.

"This is charity," the abbot returns.

Longshanks waves two soldiers forward. "Take him!" he commands.

As the abbot is seized by the arms and the tray of food drops to the ground, the monk standing closest picks it up and replaces the spilled contents.

"Do not think your robes will protect you!" Longshanks storms. "You damn yourselves by this!"

The abbot's face shows no fear. "We will be doubly damned if we stand by and do nothing while a child starves."

Longshanks' hand lashes out and smacks the abbot across the left side of his face with a ringed hand. His lip splits and blood sprays across Longshanks' arm. Even the soldiers holding the abbot blanch at the surprising anger.

Longshanks is trembling uncontrollably now. His breath comes in short rasps. It sounds like two pieces of slate being ground together.

A murmur of protest rises up from the villagers, a low growling. The soldiers make a menacing move toward them, then stop. For all their weapons, the soldiers know they are outnumbered.

For a moment it is as if the entire scene has frozen, like a landscape locked in a sudden grip of ice. Only Longshanks' eyes seem to move and they swivel toward me.

"It is you," he seems to be saying, "who holds the fate of these villagers."

I look away, then back again, and still he stares.

I cannot think what to do or say. The villagers, the monks have gathered here because of me. I understand that. But to do what Longshanks wills would be a betrayal of their courage. Yet to let them throw their lives away because of me . . .

The choice is too hard.

Dear Lord, I think, have mercy on us all.

Then I lower my head and say nothing. Which is, I suppose, a kind of choice.

The stillness of the moment stretches on and on till I think perhaps I am already dead. But when I raise my eyes, everyone is still here.

However Longshanks is no longer looking at me. He is addressing his captain.

"Give the key to the abbot," he says, his voice old and defeated.

"But, sire—" the captain begins.

Longshanks cuts him off with a decisive chop of his hand. "Do as I say, damn you! The girl will not yield to me while she lives and if she dies, she may . . . she may . . ."

His voice shrivels away as he peers about him. Is he seeing ghosts by my cage? I look where he is looking. All I see are friends.

Longshanks turns his sternest gaze upon the abbot. "Do with her as you will, but see that she does not escape or I will have your head. *This* I promise."

The abbot bows obediently and holds that position while Longshanks staggers back to his litter. No one dares offer him a hand. He climbs in and gives the command to return to the priory.

Thrusting the key at the abbot, the captain makes a face and turns away. This is an act of weakness that he wants no part of. His soldiers release the abbot, who walks over to the cage, his head high. His broken lip has already crusted over.

Everything has suddenly become blurred and I lie back and close my eyes. I have saved the folk of Lanercost, I think. I have saved them all.

When the key grates in the lock, it is a sound at once so harsh and sweet, I have to bite my poor cracked lips to keep from crying. And when the door swings open, I am reminded of the stone being rolled away from the cave where Christ was laid.

"Come, brothers," the abbot says. "Carry the child into the spittal. Gently, now. Gently. Brother Luke, prepare a bed for her. With our softest linens, lest they bruise her wasted limbs. Brother Theo, fetch fresh water and a cloth. I am certain we will find a woman from the village who will come and tend her."

I open my eyes again and see three women step forward. One of them is Lady Enid.

My chaplain, Brother Quintus, leans over me as gentle arms pick me up from the floor of the cage. For the first time he is smiling.

I try to smile back but it hurts too much.

"Am I . . . going . . . to die?" I manage to ask with my last bit of breath.

"No," says Brother Quintus. "Clearly God will not let you. He has—it seems—other plans."

The king is dead.

So Enid tells me. She is the one person allowed to speak to me here at Watton Nunnery, and she never lies. She has not the guile for it.

When I was moved from Lanercost, I was allowed to take a single attendant with me. Enid begged to come and the abbot arranged with her family that she should. So now she is my serving lady in truth, just as I promised she should be.

But she is more than that. She is my window on the world. Through all these months she has been listening to the gossip among the sisters and picking up what news she can when she runs errands into town. She passes it all on to me so that I know the world still exists beyond these high convent walls.

The king is dead.

If Enid had meant my father, she would have named him Robert the Bruce. Much as she loves me, Enid is not quite ready to think of Father as a king.

She means Edward Longshanks, of course. King of England. He is dead some three miles from Carlisle, still pursuing his war. Dead of the disease that ate him up from within.

This news has been a long year coming for me, a year in

which I have been shut up in this Gilbertine nunnery, far from home.

God's prisoner. That is what the nuns called me when I first arrived. Perhaps they meant it kindly. He is certainly a more merciful gaoler than Longshanks.

The nuns treat me well enough. I have plain food but there is plenty of it. And a hard bed but no harder than a cage floor. I have blankets to keep me warm.

Yes, they treat me well enough, but they are still my guards. They are forbidden to discuss anything with me concerning events in Scotland. Above all they are forbidden to make any mention of my father.

Mother Superior made that clear from the moment I walked through the nunnery's doors. She looked down her exceedingly long nose at me and rattled her beads. "If you persist in asking questions, you will receive no answer. And then you will be placed in the smallest, coldest cell in the convent and the door will be kept locked." Her voice was so icy, I had no doubt of it.

"But," she added, though her eyes and mouth were not a whit warmer saying it, "if you ask no questions, you will have the freedom of the chapel, the orchard, and the gardens." She shook her finger under my nose, then turned and walked away. Her grey skirts made a swishing sound, like broomstraws on the stone floor.

The thought of being able to walk in the orchard and gardens after those weeks in the cage made me keep my tongue. They became my sanctuary.

I also volunteered to help in the kitchen. It gives me some means of passing the time other than in embroidery or walking or prayer. I am learning quite a lot about making bread, pastries, and pies. My gooseberry tarts are quite accomplished.

But pies and bread and gooseberry tarts cannot compete with the news Enid has brought me today. She whispers as she passes me a bowl of stew, "The king is dead." Then we take a long walk in the gardens and she holds my hand and tells me the rest.

Even in the end, Longshanks hated my country. It seems he urged his son to boil the flesh from his bones and place the bones in a casket to be carried along at the head of the army. "No one," he supposedly said, "will overcome you whilst you have my bones borne with you."

If I close my eyes, I can hear his voice saying that. He hisses as he speaks, like a serpent.

Enid adds, "Little Edward be not brave enough to do the deed." She giggles. "He be whey-faced and squeamish like. Brought his Da's body home for a decent and proper burial."

I do not say what I want to. That I find it fitting that Longshanks has died before me. Some secrets I keep, even from Enid.

But, oh, the others Longshanks took before he died. I think of them often.

Uncle Neil, good old Atholl, Aunt Christina's lovely husband Christopher Seton, Uncle Thomas, and Uncle Alexander, all painfully executed: hanged, drawn, and quartered, their heads cut off and set on pikes. Bishops Lamberton and Wishart and the Abbot of Scone carried south in chains. All, all victims of Longshanks' horrible spleen. Enid has brought me news of them. And of Christina and Mother Elizabeth, prisoners in far-off nunneries. And Isabel and Mary still hung up in cages off the battlements of Berwick and Roxburgh castles.

But Father is free, and with him Scotland's freedom that all my loved ones have died fighting for.

Enid and I walk back inside and she leaves me. I go to my room alone.

Has it been worth it?

I ask myself this question every day.

But this very hour I have my answer. Looking up into the corner of my bare little room, I see a spider that has escaped Enid's dust mop. It is desperately trying to anchor its web with a skein of silk. Again and again it hurls itself into the air, carrying its tiny rope.

As I watch it, I think to myself that Father, like that spider, will never give up. He will keep flinging himself again and again against the English might. He will fight on, whatever the cost, until our kingdom is finally free.

If I stay true, then I may one day be reunited with him. That hope may be as thin as the spider's thread, but it's also as strong as the heart that clings to it. And that makes it stronger, much stronger, than kings or armies or stone walls—or even an iron cage.

WHAT IS TRUE ABOUT
THIS STORY

The starting point of this story is the actual decree issued by King Edward I of England that three of the ladies who had been captured at Tain should be imprisoned in cages. These were Isabel of Buchan, Robert Bruce's sister Mary, and his eleven-year-old daughter, Marjorie.

We know for a fact that Isabel and Mary were caged in Berwick and Roxburgh respectively, in cages that match the description of the one we use in our story. Orders were given for a cage to be prepared at the Tower of London to hold the young Princess Marjorie as well. In the end, Marjorie was never sent to London but was instead made a prisoner at the Gilbertine nunnery at Wotton in England.

We speculate that as the other two ladies were caged on the Scottish borders, that Edward may well have subjected Marjorie to a similar fate at Lanercost, where he lay sick. Certainly enough of an outcry was raised against his treatment of her that he abandoned the idea of removing her to London.

Edward I of England was called Longshanks because he was an enormously tall man for the period—over six and a half feet tall. He liked to refer to himself as "Hammer of the Scots," proudly, vowing to bring that proud northern nation to heel. In fact, Edward had not been a bad king for much of his reign, but after his beloved wife Eleanor died, something went wrong and the dark side of his personality took hold. He became cruel, vindictive, unceasing in his hatred of the Scottish people, and of Robert Bruce, his erstwhile friend, in particular.

In the months following the events portrayed in this book, Robert Bruce (or in the Norman French of the day, Robert de Brus) recovered from his defeat at Methven and waged a brilliant guerilla campaign against his enemies. A series of victories over the English brought the Scots flocking to his banner to oppose Edward's cruel treatment of their country. Even the Earl of Ross, who had sent the royal ladies as prisoners to England, eventually joined Bruce's cause and became one of his most loyal followers. Though history does not tell us why Ross made such a reverse, we have speculated on it with the scene between Elizabeth and her captor.

When Longshanks died in July 1307—begging his son to take his bones into battle—the weak-willed Edward II was unable to prevent Robert Bruce from establishing control over the whole of northern Scotland. The two kings finally met in battle in 1314 at Bannockburn in sight of Stirling Castle. In spite of being outnumbered three to one, Bruce inflicted a crushing defeat on his enemy that guaranteed Scotland's freedom for centuries to come.

So many English nobles were captured at Bannockburn that Bruce was finally able to ransom his family back. After eight years in captivity, Marjorie and the others made a joyful return to Scotland. Only Isabel of Buchan was not repatriated, and she disappears from history at this point. Did she die in prison? No one knows.

The following year Marjorie—now twenty—married Walter Stewart, one of the heroes of Bannockburn. She soon became pregnant. Tragically, she was badly injured in a fall from her horse and did not survive the birth of her son. He, however, went on to become King Robert II. So Marjorie's son became the first of the long line of Stewart Kings who not only ruled Scotland, but eventually became the rulers of England as well.

King Robert never forgave himself the murder of Comyn in the church. When as an old man he knew himself to be dying, he asked that his heart be taken to the Holy Land and buried there, as a sign that he begged forgiveness for the deed. The soldiers carrying the heart in a gilded and bejeweled casket were set upon and many were killed, so the stragglers returned home, where the casket was buried in a Scottish abbey.

The only real tinkering we have done with the historical facts are these: Marjorie's actual term of captivity in a cage, which is still debated by scholars; Isabel of Buchan crowning King Robert on his coronation day (she actually arrived two days later with her husband's destriers, and crowned him then). Also, Marjorie was probably not present in Dumfries right after the murder of Red Comyn. Christina is called Christian in various records, and Neil is also called Nigel. We do not know if Marjorie was called Jo by her intimates, but as that is a common Scots endearment—meaning "loved one"—we thought it appropriate.

Writing a novel is, of course, different from writing history. The storyteller fills in the interstices of the historical record with guesses and judgments. We have worked hard to stay in keeping with what is known, while still telling a stirring story.

The life of a hero like Robert Bruce inevitably becomes surrounded by legends. The most famous of these is that, while he was in hiding from his enemies, sheltering in a Highland cave, he saw a spider repeatedly working at its web in spite of setback after setback. He took this as a sign that he too must persevere if he was to achieve his goal of becoming king.

We do not know whether this spider-in-the-cave tale really happened to Bruce. Recent scholarly thought is that the incident actually happened to his lieutenant, Jamie Douglas, in a field, and simply attached to Robert's story. No one knows for sure. If it did not happen to King Robert, or Jamie Douglas, perhaps—as we have suggested here—it happened to his Marjorie. Certainly both father and daughter found the courage to survive many hardships and finally fulfill their destinies.